THE FORTUNES OF TEXAS

*Follow the lives and loves of a complex family
with a rich history and deep ties
in the Lone Star State*

HITTING THE JACKPOT

The Maloneys of Chatelaine, Texas,
have just discovered they are blood relations
to the Fortunes—which makes them instant
millionaires. But their inheritance comes with
a big secret attached that could change
everything for their small-town family...

When Isabel Banninger's blog reveals a
hidden truth about Reeve Fortune's relatives,
she doesn't expect him to thank her. But
neither does she expect a lawsuit. She vows to
keep her distance from the litigious CEO, but
when she runs out on her own wedding, it is
Reeve to the rescue in a most unexpected way!

Dear Reader,

Is there *another* Fortune?

That's the question in the back of CEO Reeve Fortune's mind that is brought front and center when he impulsively helps a beautiful bride escape her wedding before the "I dos."

Only Isabel Banninger turns out to be the popular blogger who's been speculating over his family's dirty laundry. So how can it be that he finds himself falling for her when he hides her away from the immediate fallout caused by her running out on her own society wedding?

Whether there is another Fortune or not, Isabel just knows that it's too soon for her to trust her feelings about her unexpected rescuer. How can she go so quickly from her cheating fiancé to falling for a guy she'd thought only cared about the bottom line on his balance sheet? The last thing she wants to do is make another mistake.

For these folks, *Fortune* isn't merely a name or monetary wealth. *Fortune* is finding the ones who fill your life with meaning. For Isabel and Reeve, it is realizing that all the other distractions and "stuff" are just details, and *their* hunt for fortune can only succeed by trusting their hearts.

Thank you for joining their quest!

Allison

Fortune's Runaway Bride

ALLISON LEIGH

Special thanks and acknowledgment are given to
Allison Leigh for her contribution to
The Fortunes of Texas: Hitting the Jackpot miniseries.

HARLEQUIN®

SPECIAL EDITION™

Recycling programs
for this product may
not exist in your area.

ISBN-13: 978-1-335-72467-0

Fortune's Runaway Bride

Copyright © 2023 by Harlequin Enterprises ULC

For questions and comments about the quality of this book,
please contact us at CustomerService@Harlequin.com.

Harlequin Enterprises ULC
22 Adelaide St. West, 41st Floor
Toronto, Ontario M5H 4E3, Canada
www.Harlequin.com

Printed in U.S.A.

Though her name is frequently on bestseller lists, **Allison Leigh**'s high point as a writer is hearing from readers that they laughed, cried or lost sleep while reading her books. She credits her family with great patience for the time she's parked at her computer, and for blessing her with the kind of love she wants her readers to share with the characters living in the pages of her books. Contact her at allisonleigh.com.

Visit the Author Profile page
at Harlequin.com for more titles.

For Fortune hunters everywhere.

The Chatelaine Report

I'm surrounded with well-wishers! If you've heard the rumors, they are true. The Chatelaine Report *will be going on hiatus for a few weeks while this reporter goes on her honeymoon. Tomorrow will be the most incredible June wedding with TFIII. Order-for-one will be no more. It'll be order-for-two-please from here on out for the new Mrs. Trey Fitzgerald!*

Along with sharing the details of what should be a spectacular honeymoon when I return, I'll also address the fallout after my last post, and the legal action threatened by Reeve Fortune and his big sis, Gigi. To say they did NOT like what The Chatelaine Report *said is putting it mildly...*

Chapter One

No church had ever looked so beautiful.

White flowers cascaded from every pew and loose petals artfully outlined the aisle. The occasional disarray from the sweep of the ten bridesmaids' gowns only enhanced the lovely vision.

The music from the pipe organ swelled, and the late afternoon sun streamed through the clerestory windows at just the right angle.

It had all been perfectly timed and coordinated to achieve the most perfect result.

Timing. To the minute.

Decor. White. More white.

Gowns. Lilac. Couture.

Tuxes. Black. Custom.

Visually, it was stunning.

Isabel Banninger's father stood ten paces away,

his arm at the ready to escort her up that long aisle to marry Trey Fitzgerald III. Charismatic. Handsome TFIII.

He stood at the end of the aisle wearing the tux that fit his tall, lean body to perfection. His confident, blindingly white smile was directed to the guests. To his raft of groomsmen. To her bridesmaids, arranging themselves exactly where they'd practiced just two days earlier.

Confident. That was Trey.

Everything always worked out for him.

Always.

The matron of honor—Isabel's sister Ronnie—had reached the end of the aisle and was moving into place. The guests all rose to their feet. A sea of faces turned toward her.

The music seemed to reach a fevered pitch.

Isabel took a first step and felt the hushed anticipation of the guests like a palpable thing.

Don't do this!

The thought that had been a hesitant whisper in the back of her mind suddenly eclipsed the gasp and wheeze of the pipe organ. It screamed through her head.

Unescapable. Undeniable.

She whirled, the skinny heels of her custom-dyed silk sandals slipping a little as she raced away from that confident smile.

Not always, Trey.

Not this time.

The doors slammed open under her palms and

she was out. Out onto the wide, shallow steps of the Third Community Church of Corpus Christi. Her heart hammered.

Now what?

She looked left. Cars parked nose to end all the way down the block.

She looked right. A parking lot just as full as the pews inside the church behind her.

The limousine that was to transport the newly married Mr. and Mrs. Fitzgerald on the long drive to their lavish reception at the prestigious LC Club on Lake Chatelaine was parked at the ready. But the driver was conspicuously absent.

She turned to the left again, charging blindly down the steps. She just needed to get to the end of the block. She'd duck into the convenience store and—

Do what?

The bus stop. She'd get to the bus stop and—

Do what?

Her head whirled. She'd run, but now what was she supposed to do? Where was she supposed to go? All of her family and friends were back there in the church and—

The wall came out of nowhere.

She hit it with no finesse whatsoever.

Flowers burst free from her enormous bouquet like a flock of flushed birds.

The wall's cell phone flew, too.

It dived straight to the cement.

"Sorry," she gasped. It was hard to lean over with Italian silk constricting her from breasts to knees, but she did it anyway. Light prickled behind her eyes, and she wobbled precariously, but the wall's hand caught her bare arm, keeping her from total ignominy.

"Careful there."

His deep voice barely registered as she found the hard edges of the slender phone and straightened again.

Dark suit. White shirt. Silver tie shoved haphazardly into his lapel pocket like he had every intention of putting it on but hadn't gotten around to it yet.

Probably because he'd been more interested in the picture on his cell phone.

She'd left a smear of Number 879 Red on the front of his shirt. Like he'd been nicked with a little dagger at the center of his chest.

She looked up even farther and met a pair of bluer-than-blue eyes, and she very nearly dropped the phone all over again.

Could the day get *any* worse?

"What're you doing here?"

Reeve Fortune raised an eyebrow, managing to look amused and cynical at the same time. Which, in her limited experience, seemed to be his usual expression.

"More to the point," he said, jerking his chin toward the church behind her, "what are you *not* doing in there?"

She ignored the question and pushed past him.

Since he was basically a human wall, solidly built and nearly a foot taller than her even with her treacherously high heels, he didn't move much.

She realized he hadn't taken his phone back, either.

The cracked screen did nothing to obscure the image of Trey Fitzgerald III, surrounded by his laughing groomsmen, beer mugs in their hands, raised in salute. The only thing in Trey's hands, however, was the naked woman he was kissing.

A naked woman who was most assuredly *not* his intended bride.

The social media post didn't shock Isabel. Not like it had when she'd seen it first thing that morning.

Happy wedding day to you, Isabel Banninger.

"Not marrying your *buddy*," she finally told Reeve.

He played basketball with Trey nearly every week. For all she knew, he'd been the one behind the camera.

She slapped the phone against Reeve's chest, and he barely caught it before it fell to the ground a second time. She gave him a wide berth as she tottered down another two steps.

Any minute now, Trey would come after her, and if she had to listen to another dose of his "but princess, it didn't mean anything," she would lose her mind. "It was just the guys and me having a last hurrah before you and I tie the knot," he'd said when she confronted him that morning with the evidence.

She should have called off the wedding right then.

But no. She'd let Trey convince her otherwise.

"You know me." His persuasive tone had been pitch-perfect. "I love you. You love me. Don't over-react to something that doesn't mean anything."

If this had been the only time that wasn't supposed

to mean anything, maybe she'd still be in the church, holding her father's arm as she walked toward her future as Trey's wife.

The slick sole of her shoe slipped on the cement and she stumbled yet again.

Reeve caught her arm once more but she yanked free. A few more flowers escaped.

She glared at the bouquet. The base of it was so thick she couldn't even wrap her fingers all the way around it. She wanted to throw it to the ground altogether. Maybe even grind her slippery shoe on top of it for good measure.

But she was still at the church. The church where she'd once gone to Sunday school as a child. "Tossing" a bouquet was one thing. Throwing it away was just…littering.

"I s'pose you were there last night." She pointed her bouquet accusingly. Taking the photograph and then posting it for all the world to see.

As if what he'd done to her already wasn't enough.

"Where?"

"The bachelor pa-arty." She hated that her voice hitched. It made it sound like she wanted to cry, and crying was the last thing she felt like doing.

Screaming her outrage? Closer.

"I didn't make it."

She heard a commotion behind them and didn't look back to see who was coming out of the church. It felt like forever since she'd run out, but she knew it could only have been a minute or two.

She sucked in another uneven breath that was nowhere as deep as she needed thanks to the viselike dress and kept going, even though her wrenched ankle screamed at her.

She'd deal with her parents later. And her sisters. They'd be shocked, but they'd understand. There might not be a lot of them, but the Banningers were tight. Unlike the Fitzgeralds. Most of the three hundred guests inside the church were from the groom's side of the equation, whether family or friends or business acquaintances. Yet Trey had told her some of them didn't talk for months on end.

She realized Reeve was keeping pace with her. Almost as if he expected her to fall on her butt. Or her face.

And why not? He'd already kept her from doing both.

For a guy who'd threatened to sue her for libel, he was being suspiciously solicitous.

She wrote an online community blog. Just last month he'd taken issue with something she'd written regarding his family and a letter from his lawyer had immediately arrived, warning *The Chatelaine Report* to cease and desist.

When she'd told Trey about it, he'd just laughed it off. Told her he'd take care of it with his *buddy* and not to worry.

She watched Reeve from the corner of her eye as they reached the bottom of the shallow steps.

Not worry? A few weeks ago, the company that published her blog, Stellar Productions, had been bought out by FortuneMedia. Which meant that the head of FortuneMedia—none other than the human wall named Reeve Fortune—now held her very livelihood in his hands.

If his threat of a lawsuit didn't succeed in quashing any mention of the wildly extensive Fortune family—who were movers and shakers all over the entire state of Texas—then he would put her in the unemployment line instead.

A late-model Mercedes had been parked in the loading zone, blocking her path.

No driver there, either.

Probably having a smoke around the corner with the limousine driver while they snickered over Trey's "just boys being boys" antics the night before.

She had no money with her. No cell phone. No purse. All of that was back in the bride's room at the church, and Ronnie would bring it, along with Isabel's overnight bag, to the reception. The only thing Isabel possessed besides the wedding finery she wore was her grandmother's hanky with the pretty bluebonnets embroidered in one corner that she'd tucked into her garter.

Granny Sophia had carried the hanky when she'd married Isabel's grandfather along with a book of prayers and poems that *her* mother had written. In turn, Isabel's mother had done the same thing when she'd married Isabel's father.

Isabel had planned to follow tradition. But she'd had to improvise because of the massive bouquet. She couldn't carry both.

If she'd insisted on her granny's book and a single

stemmed flower like she'd wanted, would everything
have turned out all right?

She looked over her shoulder to see how close the
pursuit might be. But Reeve's body blocked her view
and all she accomplished was hitting her hip pain-
fully against the corner of the car.

She sucked in, winced at the pinch in her ribs, and
slapped her bouquet against the offensive vehicle.

More flowers flew and she heard Reeve swear
under his breath. He grabbed the bouquet from her.
"You're dangerous with that thing." He yanked open
the passenger door of the Mercedes and tossed the
bouquet inside.

"I should have known you'd park in a loading zone.
You think you can just do anything, don't you?"

"I think you just need to be quiet and get in before
you really hurt yourself. Or do you want to go back
into the church?" He didn't wait for an answer but
pushed her down inside the car as unceremoniously
as he'd dispatched the bouquet.

She was so shocked she didn't even try to resist.
But she also could finally see the doors of the church
open.

She pulled the long veil free where it was trapped
behind her and yanked her feet inside the car while
he shoved at the mass of organza ruffles sprouting
voluminously from her knees down.

"It's like trying to smash clouds," he muttered.
Their hands knocked against each other when she
tried to help.

But she gasped when Trey appeared in the doorway of the church, and she instinctively dived out of view, leaving Reeve to deal with the problem of her dress.

It had been hard to breathe standing straight. It was even harder hunched over in the car with her forehead pressed against the soft leather of the driver's seat.

Don't see me. Don't see me. Don't see me. The chant inside her head was accompanied by the drumming of her heart.

She didn't even realize that Reeve had closed the passenger door until he opened the driver's side next to her head. He leaned down and lifted her head just enough to slide behind the wheel as nonchalantly as he pleased.

Then he let go and her head landed unceremoniously on his leg.

And there she was. In the blink of an eye. Staring up at the underside of his dashboard, feeling surrounded by the warmth and scent of him.

What was worse? This…or Trey?

He was Trey's friend. "Why are you helping me?"

His arm brushed against her shoulder as he put the car in motion. "There's got to be a rule somewhere to always help a bride on the run."

He was just as slick a talker as Trey. She started to move but his hand settled on her head.

"Hold tight," he murmured, and she nearly passed out when she realized he was rolling down his window. He braked and called out the window. "Trey!"

She knocked her head against the steering wheel when she tried lifting up. "You vile sna—"

His hand unceremoniously covered her mouth. "Be still or he'll see you," he said under his breath.

She subsided, but only because she couldn't actually sink her teeth into the palm of his hand.

He raised his voice again. "Ceremony over already or is it just running late?" His tone was easy. Buddy to buddy.

"We're delayed a few minutes," Trey called back. "Nothing to worry about. See you inside?"

She ground her teeth together. *Nothing* to worry about?

"Can't." Reeve didn't sound regretful in the least. "Business emergency. You know how it goes."

Trey laughed. Confident. As if his bride hadn't just run out on him for all the wedding guests to see. "Maybe I'll see you at the reception, then. Got a helluva party planned. It'll be worth the drive. Fireworks on the lake."

"That's what I hear," Reeve returned.

"Even the governor's coming," Trey added. "Got confirmation just this afternoon."

"Bet your dad's pleased," Reeve responded.

"You know it!"

She heard the soft whir of the window closing again. Trey's sheer nerve infuriated her. Did he intend to have the reception without her?

"Hold on," Reeve murmured for her ears only when she tried to lift her head again. "He's still in the doorway looking."

She subsided but there was still a growl building in her throat.

Reeve's thigh shifted again, and the steering wheel brushed her forehead as he turned the car. She tried to imagine herself anywhere other than where she was. Anywhere other than with this man who was *not* her friend.

"Have to say this wedding is turning out more interesting than I expected." He sounded disgustingly cheerful. "And you're safe, by the way. He's gone back inside the church."

She did growl then and peeled his fingers away from her mouth. "Glad you're amused." She angled her head, trying to avoid the steering wheel as she awkwardly scooched away from his leg.

"Didn't say it was funny. I said it was interesting."

He lifted his arm and the edge of her veil caught on his cuff link. She ruthlessly wrenched it free and with one hand on the console, managed to lever herself upright into her seat. She leaned as far away from him as she possibly could, though he didn't even seem to notice.

He was too busy grimacing at his palm as he wiped off a smear of Number 879 Red with the tie he yanked from his pocket. When he was finished, he tossed the tie in the back seat as if it were a spent tissue. "So, what made you change your mind? Didn't like the shade of Trey's tux?"

"How can you even ask that? I know you saw the picture of him." She flicked his cracked phone where it sat on the console between them. "Kissing that naked girl."

"So?" His gaze ran over her face.

She gaped. *"So?"*

He frowned slightly as he braked before turning out onto the busy street. "What's so different about this girl from the others? Trey said you two had an open arrangement."

She blinked. "He said...*what?*"

He glanced at her as if he were suddenly reevaluating something. "No arrangement, I take it," he said after a moment.

"No," she confirmed through her teeth.

He shook his head and sighed. "Always help a bride on the run."

She waited for him to say something else. Something about the lawsuit. About buying Stellar Productions. Something that would put the bow on the big black funereal ribbon wrapped around the worst day of her life.

But he didn't say anything at all.

So neither did she.

One disaster for the day was enough.

Chapter Two

The car was picking up speed and Isabel focused on her own safety belt, trying to fasten the buckle without getting her veil caught in it.

Then she wondered why she cared. It was already torn from Reeve's cuff link. And she wasn't going to want to salvage the veil for use on another day.

She shoved the clasp together with finality and let her head fall back against the headrest.

"Thank you for the escape." She couldn't help sounding stiff. "And sorry about the lipstick stains. Hopefully *you* won't have to explain them away to someone."

She was very aware that he'd left his mark, too. Namely that she couldn't get the faint scent of him out of her nose.

The drumming inside her head had subsided,

leaving her feeling exhausted. And still short of breath.

She tugged at the top of her strapless bodice, willing another centimeter of stretch from the silk, but it was useless.

Meanwhile, she realized that Reeve didn't seem to be driving with any particular destination in mind.

She'd been born and raised in Corpus Christi but hadn't lived there for the last few years. Not since taking over *The Chatelaine Report* when its previous author retired. Working for Stellar had given her the freedom to write the kinds of stories that she wanted versus being confined to a restrictive box at the media company where she'd worked since college. At the time, her friends had told her she was making the biggest mistake of her life. What sense did it make to trade living in a vibrant city for a very small town where she'd be earning even less?

Then had come the day when she'd met Trey Fitzgerald III while blogging about a fundraising event that she'd attended on Lake Chatelaine.

Suddenly, her friends didn't think she was so pitiable after all. Isabel hadn't cared what they said. She had just cared about Trey.

The car was speeding toward the distinctive Fortune Metals headquarter complex—which Reeve also ran in addition to FortuneMedia—and she half expected him to turn in the entrance when they drove past the collection of high-rises. But he didn't.

Why he cared what she said in her local news blog was a mystery. She wrote it for the entertainment of communities like Chatelaine—for the hundreds of small towns dotting the entire map of Texas. Not for the bigwigs like him who could buy and sell entire companies before they finished breakfast.

"Where are we going?" she finally asked after another five minutes of random turns.

"You tell me. This is your escape."

"An ill-planned one." She shifted in the seat, trying to get comfortable. It had nothing to do with the fine upholstery and everything to do with the boa constrictor of a dress. How had she not noticed it before now? She'd had the final fitting just three days ago and she knew she hadn't gained an ounce. If anything, the dressmaker had warned her not to lose any weight.

Wealth of curve was not something she possessed.

"I can take you home. A hotel. Whatever. Have you already moved in with Trey?"

She shuddered, never more grateful than now that she had insisted on keeping her Chatelaine apartment until after the wedding. It was nearly empty but she hadn't yet turned in her key to her landlord, Geraldine. "I still have my own apartment." She realized she was nibbling on her thumbnail and made herself stop.

Her apartment would be one of the first places Trey would check after her parents' home here in Corpus Christi. She had her own key to his showy house by Lake Chatelaine, but he surely had to know that she wouldn't head there.

"Family?"

She shook her head.

"Hotel then. Have a preference?"

"No money on me." She picked up a hank of veil, forgetting that it was caught in her seat belt buckle, and felt it tear even more. "This dress isn't made for pockets."

He made a sound she wasn't sure how to interpret. "My treat. Consider it a wedding gift."

For the wedding that would never be.

She thought about all the gifts that had already arrived—most of which were either at her parents' home or at Trey's house. It was going to be a mammoth task returning them all.

"I should've called it off this morning," she said aloud. If she had, she wouldn't be in this mess right now, driving around directionless with the man who wanted to put her out of business.

Was this Reeve's way of apologizing?

"You probably should have."

She frowned. "I wasn't asking for your opinion."

His eyebrow twitched. "You brought it up."

She pressed her lips together and looked away. The stitch in her side had grown and she shifted uncomfortably.

"What's wrong?"

"Nothing." She looked down where her legs were engulfed in a cloud of organza. Not only had Trey paid for the dress, but he'd selected it, too.

Her mother had done a respectable job of hiding her dismay over that particular point, but Isabel had known how disappointed she'd been.

"Our wedding is an *event*, princess," Trey had said

with his trademark smile. "You know my father in-
tends to be governor one day. Fitzgerald is a big name
around here. I want it to be perfect. For you, most of
all," he'd added quickly, as if that should have been
obvious.

He'd hired the wedding stylist who'd been in
charge of the overall "look" of everything from the
flowers in Isabel's bouquet to the color of her red lipstick, and a drill sergeant of a wedding coordinator to
ensure that all of those looks came to fruition. "You
just be your beautiful self and don't worry about a
single detail."

She'd been treated like a princess. Even her sisters
had said as much, and neither one had been exactly
won over by Trey, who'd seemed too good to be true.

How easily she'd gone along with it all. With the
dress. With the makeup. With the lavish ceremony
and the even more lavish reception. It was to have
been held at the LC Club, located on the shore of a
lake that was so beautiful, people from all over the
state flocked there. To vacation. To live. The limo
drive had been timed to deliver them right after sunset. Fireworks—set off from a boat in the middle of
the lake—would greet them.

Why wouldn't she have agreed to all of that? It
was fairy-tale perfect. Just as Trey—supposedly devoted to her—was supposed to be fairy-tale perfect.

But the origins of most fairy tales were decidedly
grim, she reminded herself now.

How many others thought she was just fine with
a fiancé who had other women?

The humiliation of it all burned deep.

"I guess just take me to my apartment in Chatelaine," she said wearily, and closed her eyes. She doubted that Trey would beat them there. She didn't doubt that he would look.

His pride would demand it.

She knew that much about him, at least.

Reeve immediately turned a corner, and in her mind, she imagined the closest highway entrance. No more wandering now that he had a destination in mind.

Only instead of picking up speed, he stopped altogether.

She opened her eyes again to see they'd pulled into the parking lot of a GreatStore. Ironically, she'd worked in a GreatStore during high school.

"Wait here," Reeve ordered as he exited the car.

"Where else would I go?" she asked the empty car.

She certainly wasn't going to follow him inside.

Runaway fiancée of TFIII traipses the aisles at Corpus Christi GreatStore. Film at eleven.

No thanks.

Reeve had left the car running, the air-conditioning subtly blowing.

She plucked at her bodice again, wishing like fury that she'd followed her sister's advice to have the seamstress put a hidden zipper under her arm.

But no. Isabel had had romantic notions of Trey slowly freeing the glittering crystal buttons stretching down her spine on their wedding night...

She shuddered. The thought now was nauseating.

Reeve had left his cellphone sitting in the console. She picked it up and touched the blank, cracked screen.

It came to life, showing nothing but a notification for three missed calls below the logo of FortuneMedia. She tried to get past the logo, but the phone was password-protected.

She tried a few combinations just for the heck of it and then gave up. She set the phone back where it had been. Trey wasn't the only one who'd look for her at her apartment. Her family would, too. She just wasn't sure she could survive that long before escaping the prison of her dress. She briefly fantasized taking a pair of scissors to the gown and cutting herself out of it.

Yeah, it would ruin the wildly expensive couture gown. But why should she care? Trey could add it to the cost of his "last hurrah."

Right about now, they ought to be walking back up the aisle as husband and wife.

Annoyed with herself, she glared at the store entrance, squinting in the sunlight before automatically flipping down the sun visor.

It did no good. She was too short in the seat for it to have any effect. She looked at her reflection in the small mirror on the back of the visor.

Aside from her smeared red lipstick and a few escaping strands of hair from her fancy updo of braids and whorls, her reflection showed the same unfamiliar woman the makeup artist and a hair stylist had transformed her into before she was buttoned into her dress.

The stylist had allowed Isabel's mother the honor of doing up the last two buttons. Her mom's smile had been shaky, her eyes a little tearful as she'd carefully hugged Isabel afterward despite the stylist's warning not to muss Isabel's face.

But thoughts of her mom and dad made her conscience twang. Hard. In her anxiousness to escape, all she'd done was leave them to deal with the fallout. Michael Banninger was a hospital administrator. His wife, Lydia, a onetime beauty queen and interior designer.

Isabel needed to at least call them. There had to be a phone available inside the store that she could beg the use of. The scene her appearance would make wasn't as important as making sure her family didn't worry any more than they already were.

She started to push open the car door only to see Reeve exiting from the store. He'd barely been inside ten minutes, yet he held a shopping bag in his hand.

From GreatStore.

She would have bet good money that he never stepped foot in chain stores like that. She even started to rub her eyes, sure she was seeing things, except the false eyelashes stopped her.

He opened the door and tossed the bag on her lap as he slid behind the steering wheel again. "Not high fashion, but an alternative anyway."

She opened the bag. A bright pink T-shirt and black leggings were folded neatly inside.

He hadn't gone in there for himself.

He'd gone in there for her.

Her eyes suddenly stung again.

She hadn't cried over the damning proof of Trey's unfaithfulness. She hadn't cried over the implosion of the wedding that wasn't.

But she'd cry now over a twelve-dollar T-shirt and a pair of leggings purchased for her by a man who wanted to put her out of business?

She pinched the bridge of her nose until the urge passed. "Can I use your phone, please?" Her voice still sounded husky.

He picked it up, unlocked the screen and handed it to her. "Caller ID is blocked," he warned.

She wondered why but wasn't going to deny the fact that it was a small blessing. All she needed was for her family to think she'd run off with the man they knew was trying to ruin her.

She sniffed again and quickly texted Ronnie. Isabel's elder sister had two young children and she *always* had her cell phone with her.

It's Issa. This is a friend's phone.

She grimaced. Talk about overstatement.

Tell Mom and Dad I'm fine and that I just need a little time to myself. Sorry for the mess I've caused. Will call soon and explain. Love you all.

She hit Send and handed him back the phone. "It's a long drive to Chatelaine from here."

"It's not so bad if you know where the speed traps are."

"As if you worry about speed traps."

"I get tickets the same as anyone else."

And he probably bought his way out of them the same way that Trey did.

"It's a little less time to the lake," he added.

She shook her head. The only things she knew around the lake were the LC Club and Trey's mini-mansion. "No thanks."

"I own a place there. You could use it if you need a breather. Trey's house is nowhere near it if that's your concern."

Stay at *Reeve's* home? The very idea made her recoil.

He obviously saw that, too.

"Or not," he added blandly. He gestured toward the bag on her lap. "Nobody'll see you through the windows. Get changed." Once again, he left the car running as he reached to open his door.

"Wait—"

He glanced at her, his eyebrow raised.

Reeve was not as classically handsome as Trey, but meeting that direct blue gaze of his was just too disturbing for words.

It was no wonder that half the people at the Stellar Productions office were as much atwitter over the new owner as the other half was appalled with the changes that were reportedly in store.

"I, uh, I need help with the—" She broke off and

just turned her back toward him, indicating the problem by gathering her torn veil over her shoulder.

He sat back in the seat, and there was no imagining the audible sigh he gave. "Turn a little more if you can," he finally said.

She angled herself more in the seat. Even braced, she still jumped when she felt his first touch.

"Hold still." He sounded irritable. "What are these buttons? Glass? They're freaking tiny."

"They're crystals and they're supposed to be small," she said, clenching her teeth to keep still. It was hard considering how long it took him to unfasten the first button. But finally, she felt a slight loosening.

Relieved, she dropped her head forward, holding the bodice against her breasts as it loosened even more. After the first button, he'd obviously gotten the hang of it and went more quickly. She hauled in a deep, lung-expanding breath. *Yessss.*

"How far down do you want me to go?"

Relief was quickly displaced by awkwardness. The crystal buttons ran all the way down past her butt. He'd released enough of them to her waist that she could finish the job herself no matter how much contortionism it took. "This is fine," she said quickly.

Now that she could breathe freely, she could do anything.

He made a grunting sort of sound. "Don't take all night," he warned.

"Have plans?" she asked tartly. "Maybe going to the big party this evening at the LC Club?"

He grimaced and slammed the door closed.

Isabel peered across the empty seat for several long seconds.

But the door remained closed. The side and rear windows were so darkly tinted that she could barely see through them. The windshield was another story. She could see Reeve lean back against the hood, his arms crossed.

She chewed the inside of her cheek for a minute, studying the breadth of his shoulders beneath the excellent cut of his suit jacket. Trey's suits were all custom-made, too. And the only reason his shoulders looked wide in comparison to his trim form was because of discreet shoulder padding. She doubted that was the case with Reeve.

More irritated than ever with herself, she looked at his purchases. The shirt was a size larger than she wore, but it would make changing a little easier.

In college, she and her girlfriends had spent plenty of time at the beach. They'd learned the art of changing clothes within the confines of a beach towel. She'd do the same thing now. Just beneath a hot-pink T-shirt from GreatStore.

His cell phone on the console vibrated with another message while she yanked the T-shirt over her head, veil and all since she couldn't seem to pull it off without tearing out her hair. Then beneath the shirt, she began working herself out of the wedding gown.

The sooner she succeeded, the sooner she could also get rid of Reeve Fortune.

Chapter Three

Reeve felt the faint rocking of the car and all too easily imagined Isabel Banninger—dark-haired, dark-eyed and pocket-sized—wriggling out of that terrifyingly elaborate gown.

He looked down at the ground and rubbed the back of his neck. But there was no rubbing away the sensation of grazing her lithe back as he'd worked those glassy little buttons free.

Her tawny skin had been warm. Smooth. Inviting. Just the way he'd always imagined.

But of course, she hadn't been inviting anything except needing assistance to get out of a dress that didn't suit her in more ways than one.

He rotated his head and shoved his fists into his pockets.

Where would Isabel be now if he hadn't been late because of that odd phone call from his father?

Not inside his car, that was for sure.

He could well believe she'd have gotten somewhere, even if she'd had to get there on foot. The pint-sized bride in all her wedding finery had been fueled to go.

More power to her.

Trey was a decent enough stockbroker, but Reeve had seen for himself that the guy's loyalties were more than a little fluid. It wasn't a huge surprise that he'd lied about his and Isabel's "arrangement."

The car rocked again and this time he couldn't help but look over his shoulder. He got a glimpse of a planet-sized mass of ruffles through the windshield and resolutely looked away again.

In reality, he hardly knew Isabel. The last time he'd seen her in person had been a few weeks ago when she'd stopped by the gym where he and some others, including Trey, played basketball.

She'd been obviously agitated and hadn't stayed long.

When Trey came back to the game, he'd carelessly dismissed the brief delay. If Reeve's attention hadn't been on the departing woman, Trey would have never succeeded in swiping the game ball out of Reeve's grasp to run it down the court.

"I'm finished."

He looked around to see Isabel had rolled down her window and poked out her head.

She still wore her torn veil; it sprouted from somewhere inside the hair mounded on the back of her head. He prided himself on staying far, far away from women desiring wedding veils.

But none of them had ever been Isabel Banninger.

He pushed away from the car and shrugged off his suit coat before getting back inside.

"I'll pay you for the clothes as soon as I get my purse back," she said immediately.

"Don't worry about it." He removed his cuff links and dropped them in the ashtray that was empty except for the three other pairs he'd forgotten he'd stashed there.

"I *will* worry about it." Her voice went flat. "Wouldn't want to be accused of taking advantage of a Fortune."

He rolled up his sleeves and eyed her. "Where did *that* come from?"

She just grimaced and shook her head. "Sorry. I'm—you've helped me out and I just—" She broke off and shook her head again. She was clearly struggling for words. "I pay my own bills," she finally muttered.

"Fine," he said, more annoyed with himself than he was with her. He should have thought about shoes for her, too, and he hadn't. He'd grabbed the first items of ladies' clothes that he'd come to inside the store. "Twenty-two dollars, seventy-two cents."

The T-shirt fit her loosely, but only reminded him that if she hadn't worn a stitch beneath her strapless wedding gown, she wasn't wearing a stitch now beneath the bright pink top.

He was thirty-seven years old. Too old to be wishing that the T-shirt fit as snugly as the black leggings that ended just below her knees.

He yanked at his collar, freeing another button. "Do you need some help there or something?"

She pulled a long, braided skein of deep brown hair free and dropped it on her lap. "You think?" Her voice was tart.

He should have realized that not all of those twists and turns of hair were real. When she'd interrupted the basketball game, her hair had been as glossy and dark as a wet seal, but just past her shoulders. Same as it had been the first time they'd met nearly a year ago.

He whirled his finger in the air between them. "Turn around again."

She presented her narrow back toward him. The layers of filmy white veil puddled on the seat around her.

He'd taken down a woman's hair before plenty of times. And always as a prelude to sex.

Which was as far from the current agenda as it could possibly be.

Didn't stop him from thinking about it, though.

If he'd been better friends with Trey, he would've felt guilty. Maybe.

But Trey was just someone on Reeve's weekly pickup game who was occasionally convenient to handle an investment or two. Socially, they ran in similar circles, but that was it. Reeve had more real connections to Trey's father, Trace.

Which didn't mean Reeve intended on doing anything about Isabel. Barely an hour had passed since she'd run out on her wedding. He didn't pretend that magically meant she was available, whether he wished it or not.

He gingerly moved some of the filmy fabric to one side.

Her shoulders wiggled a little as she drew up one leg and sat on it. "I'm afraid the hairstylist might've sewn the veil into my hair," she warned with a wave of her hand.

On her middle finger, she wore a thin gold band with an infinity twist in the center. The delicate, simplistic design suited her a lot more than the gigantic diamond on her ring finger that sent prisms dancing around the car interior.

He cleared his throat again and touched one of the thin braided twists circling through gleaming brown curls. "I doubt he cares about her." He traced his finger along the braid, trying to find an end. "Trey," he added, as if there might be some doubt.

"Is that supposed to make it okay?"

He shook his head. Which, naturally, she didn't see. "No." He felt the hard edge of a tiny hairpin and carefully tugged it free. The braid came loose.

If he hadn't already known she'd been using hairpieces, he'd have been startled.

She dropped it on her lap with the other. After freeing two more braids he finally reached the point where the veil was tightly attached with a few million hairpins.

"Not sewn in," he said, finally working it free. "But damn close." He handed her the veil.

Looking solemn, she wound the damaged fabric into a loose coil and set it behind her where it was swallowed into the abyss of ruffles. "Thank you." She thrust her fingers into her hair, rubbing furiously for a couple seconds.

When she was finished, more hairpins were scattered all over his console and her lap. And her hair was left a halo of curls—half pinned up and half not.

She still dropped her head back against the headrest. Her faintly pouty lips were smiling slightly. "Relief."

He smiled slightly, too.

It was impossible not to.

Even a faint smile from Isabel Banninger was hard to resist.

She began collecting the pins, dropping them in the center of a white-and-blue hanky that she pulled out of nowhere.

"Sorry I didn't think to get you shoes."

"It's a relief knowing that you don't have every angle covered at every moment." As if he'd prompted her, Isabel began unfastening the slim satiny straps wound around her feet. Her toenails were painted a tasteful pale pink. Same as her fingernails. Only her lips had been a deep, commanding red.

His French-born mother was the only woman he knew who could carry off red lips like that.

Probably the reason why he'd never cared for the style. He'd learned very young that a kiss from Delphine Fortune meant a smear of red on his cheek and the knowledge that his *maman* was leaving again.

He put the car in gear. His vision in the rearview mirror was partially obscured by the mounds of her wedding dress.

It was a surprising choice of gown. Every other time he'd seen Isabel, her clothing had been as casually elegant and understated as his sister's. He might not always get along with Gigi, but there was no denying her excellent taste.

He didn't know anything about wedding gowns, but it was obviously expensive. And on Isabel's petite form, it had seemed entirely out of scale.

She'd managed to escape the high-heeled sandals and she drew up her legs, crossing them like some kid.

But she was a grown woman.

Her chin was pointed. Her mouth a little too wide and her nose a little too short. She was both gamine and sultry and being attracted to her was no more useful now than it had been the first time Trey had introduced her as his fiancée.

Reeve had just gotten on the highway when his phone buzzed. The car's system took it over and he glanced at the screen. His father again. It was three in the morning in France.

Philip Fortune Jr.—PJ to Reeve—was being unusually insistent. If Reeve hadn't already talked to him earlier, he would have been worried. His folks didn't make a habit of staying in touch with their younger child. They didn't make a habit of staying in touch with Gigi all that much, either.

His parents had devotion, but it was entirely between the two of them. It had never dribbled over to their own children.

He declined the call and glanced at Isabel again. She was pressing the hanky-wrapped bundle of clips against her rosy lips, her expression distant.

"Where's your apartment in Chatelaine?" he asked her.

"Around the corner from Stellar Productions." She dropped her hand to her lap and unwound her crossed legs only to shift and fold them beneath her to one side. The position left her leaning against the passenger door.

She couldn't have put more distance between them if she tried.

"I know Stellar," he said. "I don't remember an apartment building nearby." He focused on the road again, but not before seeing the way her lips compressed.

"You will when you raze Stellar's building to the ground."

His grip tightened on the steering wheel. Gigi had given him hell after overhearing his facilities director's comment that he'd be better off tearing the building to the ground than trying to rehab it. Julia Chalmers was not known for being subtle. Everyone present at the quaint old house that was used as the company headquarters had heard her comments.

"I'm not—" He broke off and shot Isabel a look.

"What do you know about me and Stellar Productions?"

She raised her eyebrows. "I know that FortuneMedia bought it out. Everyone who lives in Chatelaine knows about it." She smiled thinly. Almost goadingly. "*The Chatelaine Report* was the first place to break the news."

That annoying blog, he thought. Gigi had been pissed with him about that one, too, but for different reasons.

He was fed up with pretenders trying to feed off the Fortune name, and when *The Chatelaine Report* had started spouting Mariana Sanchez's claim that she was related to his family, he'd told his legal team to shut it down.

He'd already spent more than a year fighting the latest false claim against his great-grandfather's estate. He had no intention of wasting another year on Sanchez and hadn't wanted her efforts publicized even in an online blog with an underwhelming readership. His legal department sent a letter of warning and that was that.

His sister, Gigi, on the other hand, had taken his purchase of the company that also produced her podcast as an unwelcome inroad into her territory.

Isn't it enough that Grampy handed you the keys to Fortune Metals? You have to take Stellar Productions, too?

"*The Chatelaine Report* doesn't know everything," he told Isabel. There was no byline on the blog. For all he knew, it was written by the rotating crop of volunteers who showed up at the Stellar building every afternoon around 3:00 p.m. Just when a plate of warm cookies always magically appeared in the lobby.

"My facilities director was the one who said it'd be easier to demo the Stellar building and start from scratch. *I* didn't say it was going to happen."

"Did you say it wasn't?"

"Yeah, in a private conversation two days later when I met with Julia ag—" He broke off when his phone rang yet again. "Sorry." He hit the button to answer. "PJ, I'm driving. I'll call you back later."

"You said that before." His father's voice sounded only slightly distant. Despite living in France since his early retirement from Fortune Metals, Philip Jr.'s Texas twang was as pronounced as ever. "Did you find the journal yet?"

Reeve's patience was shorter than usual. "You just asked about it today. I haven't had a chance to look." That wasn't strictly true, but he didn't care. "I'll get back to you." Maybe in a year. Since that's about how long a stretch usually went between calls from his parents. Not waiting for a response, he ended the call again.

He looked at Isabel. She was bumping her chin with that hanky-wrapped pack of pins again, her lips downturned.

She was thinking about Trey. He'd bet his life on it.

The brief conversation with his father had at least spawned one helpful idea. "You don't really want to go to your apartment."

Her gaze slid his way. "No, but I'm going to have to, sooner or later." She sighed faintly.

"I have an idea that'll give you a little breathing space before you have to face it all."

"It" being the fallout of leaving TFIII at the altar.

Instead of looking relieved, though, she gave him a suspicious look. "Seriously. *Why* are you doing this? And don't—" she raised her hand and that big diamond flashed again "—give me another line about rules and rescues."

The only thing he'd ever rescued were business deals.

While his great-grandfather was bestowing affection on Gigi, he'd been drilling family responsibility into Reeve. And for Walter Fortune, family responsibility was inseparable from the family business. His son, Philip Fortune Sr., had been equally devoted to the business. It was only Philip Jr. who'd seemed to flunk the lessons.

After PJ had nearly squandered away the company before walking away altogether, it had taken Reeve until he was thirty years old to feel entirely secure in the family's hold on Fortune Metals.

That was seven years ago, but Reeve still blamed his father for those wasted years. His sister blamed their parents more for their lack of attention.

Turns out she'd blamed Reeve for a few things, too.

Even though lately things had improved—helped considerably by Reeve giving her a seat on the Fortune Metals board of directors—Gigi still accused him of being too focused on the bottom line. Her recent engagement to Harrison Vasquez hadn't changed *that* at all.

Reeve plucked at the lipstick stain across his shirt. "I strike you as someone who'd drive past a person stranded in the middle of nowhere, do I?"

Isabel rolled her eyes. "I wasn't stranded in the middle of nowhere."

"Metaphorically—"

"—and you might if you wanted to put them out of business!"

"I acquire businesses to keep them *in* business."

"And cut out whatever doesn't suit you."

"If it's deadweight." It wasn't something that needed an apology. But he had the strangest sensation that he'd lost control of the conversation. "Do you want to know my idea or don't you?"

She watched him through narrowed eyes. Then she gave a capitulating shrug and looked out the side window again. "Will I have to see anyone or answer any questions?"

"Not if you don't want to."

"Then fine."

It was hardly an overwhelming show of enthusiasm.

But then again, she'd escaped marrying Trey Fitzgerald. Reeve glanced at the reflection of her wedding dress in his rearview mirror.

For now.

Chapter Four

Isabel breathed easier when Reeve's car flew right past Lake Chatelaine once they reached it. He'd been right about making good time. The clouds on the horizon were beginning to hint at the colors of what would be a spectacular sunset.

She hadn't been entirely sure his "idea" wouldn't somehow involve the exclusive enclave where the LC Club was located. Not that the lake itself was owned by anyone.

But unless you were a member of the club positioned at the point of the egg-shaped lake, or owned one of the million-dollar estates nearby it, you were mostly relegated to the far shore of the lake if you were looking for a retreat on the water. That's where the boat ramp didn't cost anything, and the parking lot was wherever you happened to find a tree to park under—if you wanted shade on a hot summer day.

If you didn't care about lake access or inflated prices, the shoreline walk that stretched nearly halfway around the large lake was available for anyone and everyone.

Until Isabel had gotten involved with Trey, she hadn't spent a lot of time at the lake where people like him wanted the exclusive getaway address. Was that also Reeve's excuse for owning a place by the lake?

Given the two major companies that he ran, it was a wonder he had time for getaways at all.

He turned off the highway shortly after the glittering lake was no longer in sight and she tensed a little, because they were now on the local road that led from the lake to the town of Chatelaine.

Did it really matter if he'd tired of whatever had motivated him to help her and he just dumped her off there? In Chatelaine, a person could get anywhere they wanted on foot if they needed.

She resolutely unfolded her legs and felt for her high-heeled wedding sandals with her toes. In preparation.

But he never even reached the lone gas pump at the filling station marking the outskirts of Chatelaine.

Instead, he turned off Old Lake Road and onto a graveled one that made her wince a little in concern for his fancy car. The road wasn't marked with a signpost, but she knew that it led to a played-out silver mine that was closed except for a gift shop and weekend tours. She'd met the gift shop owner several months ago when they'd been having a special deal on custom-designed silver jewelry.

Maybe she'd have the ring she'd gotten for Trey melted right back down again.

"You know where you're going, right?"

"*I* do." He looked her way, clearly noting the way she was searching out her shoes. "Do you?"

The short answer was no, which she had to admit when he turned yet again onto another unmarked road that undoubtedly led to another abandoned mine. There were two things around Chatelaine. Ranches and old mines. The largest and longest-lived one had been owned by the Fortune Mining Company, which had later become Fortune Metals.

And which Reeve now ran.

Because being the CEO of one company wasn't enough for some people, Reeve Fortune had to be in charge of two. Fortune Metals and FortuneMedia. Both of which did business well beyond the borders of Texas.

The car bumped and jounced over the mounds of weeds separated by equally deep ruts. "Haven't been out here in a couple years," he admitted. "This is a shortcut, but I didn't know the road had gotten so bad. Probably should have come in through the main entrance. The road's private and maintained but there's a security gate." He gave her a glance. "It's monitored."

She appreciated his discretion, but she was still glad to know he had a working cell phone. She wasn't confident that his car wouldn't get stuck on his so-called shortcut. Walking down a cracked sidewalk from one block to the other in Chatelaine was very different from finding their way on foot from the back of beyond to civilization.

But they didn't get stuck.

And soon he'd crested a small rise that offered a panoramic view of the countryside. Wild, windblown grasses. Stubby brush and a row of enormous oak trees. Enhanced by the deepening golden sunlight, it was everything that she found beautiful about this corner of the world.

The three cone-shaped turrets just visible through the trees, though, was jarring. She sat forward to stare out the windshield more closely. "Is that the *castle*?"

She'd only heard talk of the mysterious castle since she'd moved to Chatelaine. Isabel didn't know a single soul who'd ever seen the inside of it. Not even her elderly landlord, who'd lived in Chatelaine her entire life and seemed to know everything about everyone. Geraldine said it was falling apart in ruin. Bianca Sellers, who lived in the apartment next to Isabel, said it was abandoned. Seanmarie, who worked a few hours a week as receptionist at Stellar Productions, said it was haunted by the millionaire eccentric who'd built it.

He gave a wry grunt. "It was my great-great-uncle's house. Wendell Fortune."

She startled. She'd heard the name before, but only because she'd blogged a few times about the windfalls some of Chatelaine's bachelors had experienced in the last several months. Windfalls that had come from learning that their grandfather was none other than Wendell Fortune. "Doesn't he have family there now?" she asked cautiously.

"No." He didn't seem inclined to elaborate.

Maybe he didn't like knowing that he had cousins who'd been getting whopping huge checks from the Fortune coffers, cousins who were just as ordinary as Isabel was. The Maloney brothers hadn't grown up with private schools and nannies the way Reeve had. And even though the brothers now went by *Fortune* Maloney, she was pretty certain they still didn't call a castle a house or consider one to be a normal part of everyday life.

She folded her arms, stewing while Reeve drove in and out of the shadows cast by the enormous trees until a narrow, paved road bisected the rocky, uneven lane they were on.

The main road, she assumed.

He turned onto it, picking up speed, and the castle loomed larger and larger until it nearly consumed her entire field of vision.

When he reached the wide expanse of shrubs running all the way around the front of the structure that prevented them getting any closer, Reeve parked and turned off his engine. She felt his glance but couldn't do anything other than stare through the car windows at the castle.

The place was unbelievable.

Like something built centuries ago. There were even flying buttresses, complete with gargoyles, no less. She'd have to tell Geraldine it most definitely was not a ruin.

"I'm surprised there's not a drawbridge," she told Reeve. There was no water for a bridge to span. But the bushes strongly reminded her of a moat, nonetheless. "Why on earth is this *here*?"

"Because this area is where Wendell lived," he said drily. "So did his big brother—my great-grandfather, Walter Fortune. Their family owned the Chatelaine Silver Mine and—" he gestured at the castle "—you can see how profitable it was."

"What kind of house did *your* great-grandfather have? Another abandoned castle?"

He smiled faintly. "Walter called this place Wendell's Folly." He pushed open his door. "And it isn't quite abandoned. But nobody will find you here. I guarantee that. People are rarely allowed inside."

She noticed he didn't answer about his great-grandfather's house. "When they are, are they allowed back outside again?"

His smile was sudden but brief.

It still knocked her for a loop and she quickly focused on the many straps of her sandals as he rounded the vehicle.

She was still fastening the tiny buckles around her ankles when he opened her door for her. He waited until she'd finished, and she took the hand he offered as she climbed from the vehicle.

As soon as she had her footing, though, she let go again. She didn't even know she'd rubbed her palm against her hip until she felt his gaze watching her.

She dropped her hand and gingerly started forward, trying to keep the heels of her shoes from sinking into the dirt, but it was impossible. She probably looked ridiculous. T-shirt and leggings and custom-dyed shoes with crystal flowers on the toes, but it was the shoes or nothing.

And this definitely was not the place to try going barefoot, no matter how tender her ankle still felt. It was too easy imagining snakes lurking under the bushes.

"But why a *castle*?" she asked. Chatelaine was, primarily, a ranching community. The norm were farmhouses that ran the gamut from small and exceedingly spare to occasionally ostentatious.

This multistory behemoth, compete with towers and turrets and a bazillion mullioned windows reflecting the orange and red sky, was something entirely different.

He didn't head toward the grandiose front entrance directly across from them, but instead walked slowly, in unexpected deference to her, along the perimeter of the shrubbery-moat. "Everything I know about the place and about Wendell, I learned from reading my great-grandfather's journals. Wendell spent a lot of time traveling in Europe and ended up with a strong interest in architecture. Strong enough to build his own Texas version of a castle."

"Looks...atmospheric."

"Creepy, you mean? Wait until you meet the ghosts."

She knew he was pulling her leg. That alone was more unsettling than the idea of ghosts, which she didn't believe in anyway.

Eventually, they reached a break in the spiky

bushes allowing them to reach the cobblestones on the other side. Walking on the uneven stones was no easier than the dirt, though, and when her heel caught for a second time, he grabbed her arm and didn't let go until she stopped to study a cornerstone as they passed it.

She traced the granite bas-relief of a centaur and studied the raised engravings of vine-entwined ovals that worked all the way from the foundation to a stained-glass window at least three stories up. The design was both decorative and disturbing, and she couldn't quite decide why.

She tapped the centaur's head and skipped unevenly to catch up with Reeve again. "You said it wasn't quite abandoned. What does that mean?"

"Just that nobody has lived here since Wendell. But instead of turning it into a museum or selling it—though why anyone would want to buy a castle that looks more suited for a Scottish moor than Texas beats me—the family has continued holding on to it. Maintaining it."

"So if it were up to you, you'd get rid of it?" She couldn't help wondering what sort of claim Wendell's newfound grandchildren had on the castle. Or if they had any claim at all.

"I'm as bad as everyone else," Reeve was saying. "Can't bring myself to push the issue."

"Different standards for a Fortune castle and an old house in Chatelaine, I guess."

He sighed loudly. "For the last time, I'm *not* tear-

ing down the Stellar building. Do I have to take out
an ad to get it through people's heads?"

Maybe *The Chatelaine Report* could blog about
it, she thought waspishly, but had the good sense not
to say it.

"The Stellar building at least has a purpose," he
continued, much to her surprise. "More so than this
place, at any rate. There's a caretaker who checks up
on things periodically. Usually at night. He's kind
of an odd duck. Stays out of sight whenever people
are around."

"Isn't that counterproductive for a caretaker?"
They finally stopped again in front of another door—
this one considerably more prosaic in appearance than
the main entrance. Situated in a small alcove, it was
just a flat slab of weathered dark wood with a heavy-
looking latch and a faded cast-iron door knocker.

"Give him a pass. Smitty's been around since my
father's reign." He reached up with both hands to feel
above the wide stone ledge above the door and she
assumed he was looking for a hidden key. But instead, he hitched himself straight up off the ground
until he could prop his gleaming leather shoe on the
thick door latch. Then he heaved himself all the way
up until he was standing on the ledge.

All she could do was stare. Not just over the speed
at which he'd accomplished his spiderlike feat, but the
fact that he'd done it at all.

"*What* are you doing?"

He inched several feet to the left and pushed at the

corner of the tall mullioned window. It tilted inward. "Getting inside. Same way I've been doing since I was sixteen." He flashed that brief smile again and disappeared through the narrow opening.

What other surprises was he hiding under his bespoke suit?

She shook the thought out of her head and glanced around.

There wasn't exactly anyone around to witness Reeve's odd mode of entry—only the orange striation of clouds growing more colorful by the minute, fulfilling the promise of a typically magnificent June sunset.

Maybe this was just one long, terribly vivid dream.

Her fiancé hadn't cheated on her the night before their wedding. She would wake up and be thrilled to be marrying the man of her dreams. Reeve Fortune would be merely a guest—probably late—sitting in the pews when the minister pronounced the new husband and wife.

She ran her hand over the stone next to the door. It was sharp and rough and abrasive enough to scrape her skin.

She definitely was not dreaming.

Then the door suddenly opened from the inside and Reeve stood there.

His light brown hair was disheveled, and a line of dirt had joined the smear of Number 879 Red across his chest. He sketched a mocking bow and held out his palm. "Welcome to Wendell's Folly."

Reeve Fortune was a captain of industry, she reminded herself. Not a madman who squirreled away runaway brides in mysterious Texas castles.

Even if he *had* called her blog libelous.

She glanced around once more. At the increasingly brilliant sunset. At the heavy engraving that surrounded the doorframe with the same pattern she'd seen before.

It all felt very odd. Surreal.

Yet better than the alternative that she had left standing in a church miles and miles away.

She set her fingertips against Reeve's palm, absently noticing a ridge of calluses. They were as unexpected as everything else about him. "Thank you."

Then she stepped inside, and a sudden guest of wind made the door slam heavily behind her.

Chapter Five

Once the echo of the slamming door faded, the silence inside the house was deep and thick.

Isabel was annoyed with the shiver squiggling down her spine and deliberately focused on her surroundings. Namely the fact that the door had opened into an entirely empty room. It was about twenty feet square and lined with shelves that stretched up the walls. The only thing on them appeared to be a thick layer of dust. She looked up at the window through which he'd entered. It was a good ten-foot drop.

She supposed he could have used a ladder and stored it away before opening the door for her, but why hide it?

"There's a market for people who pay good money to spend the night in creepy castles." She folded her arms over her chest and rubbed her arms. The day had been warm but the temperature inside the thick walls was downright chilly. "Maybe that would provide an acceptable reason for keeping a castle. A whole new stream of revenue." As if he needed it.

His lips twitched. "I'll keep it in mind. Meanwhile, do you want to get off that foot you're pretending is fine, or have the ten-cent tour? It won't seem eerie after you've seen the place."

She'd have to withhold judgment on that. "Tour please. And I'm not limping." Much.

He gave her a disbelieving look but said no more.

She followed him from the room and along a stone-floored hallway illuminated only by the rosy light shining through the windows high above their heads.

"Are you *sure* we're not trespassing?" It was just too weird to enter the castle the way they had.

"Can't trespass on what I—at least my family and I—already own. The castle belongs to the Fortune Trust."

She didn't really know a lot about trusts but supposed that was the reason why Wendell's grandchildren hadn't already taken it over.

Still…she gave him a suspicious look. "Why don't you have a key, then?"

He gave a short laugh. "Want me to carry a key for every property I own?"

The image of him with an enormous ring holding hundreds of keys did seem ridiculous.

Then he pushed open a swinging door that let out a shrieking squeak of protest.

Her mind immediately scurried back to scary mov-

ies and the foolish characters who walked straight
into danger.

Only nothing on the other side of the door looked
dangerous. In fact, it was an entirely ordinary, albeit
very dated, kitchen illuminated by three light bulbs
hanging down from the ceiling on a thick black cord.

The square linoleum table had four chairs. The
farmhouse sink came from the days when it had been
the norm and not a decor choice. The white refrigera-
tor looked like it was straight out of the fifties, as did
the electric stove and the wall oven. The only thing
that struck her as odd was the absence of windows.

Maybe castle kitchens weren't supposed to have
windows. Might prove too distracting for the souls
slaving away to feed the mighty of the house.

Considering how extravagant the exterior of the
castle had been, she actually felt disappointed. "This
is it?"

"What'd you expect?"

"I don't know. Double ovens at the very least."

He smiled faintly. "This isn't the main kitchen. I
think it was originally meant for the housekeeper's
personal use. But everything in here still works." As
if to prove it, he turned the small dial on a transistor
radio that sat on the pale green–tinted countertop.
Immediately, tinny music began playing.

"My grandpa used to have a radio like that in his
woodshop." Turning on an ancient radio was one
thing. But she doubted that Reeve had much personal
experience using the rest of the kitchen appliances.

It was difficult imagining him standing at any stove, much less this one, cooking a meal for himself.

But then again, she hadn't expected him to scale a wall, either.

He turned off the radio and pushed open another swinging door opposite the first one, and she followed him through. Unlike its mate, the hinges were mostly quiet when he released it.

They passed through a long room—clearly a dining room despite the sheets shrouding every piece of furniture—and into another narrow hallway. Her high heels tapped loudly in the silence as she followed him around odd corners and through more furniture-shrouded rooms until he pushed open a door and ushered her through.

She stopped in her tracks and felt her jaw slack. "Good...grief."

A sea of gleaming black and white marble tiles laid in a checkerboard fashion covered the floor in what was obviously the castle's main foyer. She looked one way to the massive wood entry door and then the other way to the impressively wide staircase that disappeared beyond a massive shadowy arch. There were other arches as well. As casing for a half dozen closed doors on the right side of the wide space and in the windows a full story up on the left.

She craned her head back, circling slowly as she took in the brilliantly colored mural of birds that covered the high ceiling. She swayed, feeling a little dizzy.

"You all right?"

"Yeah." She looked over at Reeve. "I suppose this is all pretty ordinary for you."

"Sure," he said, looking amused. "I have canaries painted on all my ceilings." He pushed open one set of the double doors and stepped back. "The great hall," he said.

She walked past him into the room.

Great was definitely the appropriate term. The ceilings were even higher than the entry. Even though Isabel had never visited Europe, she imagined it had a European flavor to it. Like some old Gothic church with cathedral-height trusses, gold-leaf beams and even more painted murals on the ceiling that were reflected in the near-mirror shine of the white marble floor. It was beautiful. And as empty as that first storage room had been.

"Put up half a dozen basketball hoops, and you could have a tournament in here."

Why had she said that?

Basketball made her think of Trey.

She rubbed her arms again.

"I don't know if this room was ever used for anything," Reeve admitted. He touched the small of her back briefly and she moved out of the way so he could pull the door closed again.

"You seem to know the place well."

"I've done my share of exploring." He gestured carelessly toward the staircase. "I've only gone up there once."

She goggled. "Why?"

"It's just more of the same. When you've seen one

marble bust, you've seen 'em all. Plus this side of the castle is—" He shook his head. "I don't know. Too fussy for my tastes. I like the rooms in the wing we came through."

"Despite the sheets all over everything."

His lips twitched. "Despite them. First time I came here was with my great-grandfather."

"Not your uncle?"

He shook his head. "Never met him. As far as I can tell, he preferred living abroad over the United States. My opinion about the castle was influenced by Walter. The only time he brought me here, we came through that same side door. I never even saw this side of the castle until after he died."

She ran her fingers along the rounded edge of a glass-topped table in the middle of the foyer. Like everything else, the base of it was far from ordinary— three knights in armor on bended knee. Another suit of armor—full size—stood in an alcove beyond the staircase keeping company with a half dozen busts placed on large pedestals. Despite the dust she'd seen elsewhere, here there seemed to be none. The reclusive caretaker clearly picked and chose where attention was given.

She followed Reeve back through the interior doorway they'd come through.

The gray stone floor seemed particularly drab after the visually stunning marble checkerboard. And the cement walls were almost monastic in comparison to the opulent artwork and murals. They went through yet another doorway and down another hall. Even more narrow. Even dimmer.

She shivered and focused less on the moody atmosphere and more on the midpoint between his substantive shoulders. "Seems sad. Your uncle spent the time to build something like this, but preferred living elsewhere? Maybe his efforts didn't live up to his expectations."

"Maybe." Reeve pushed open yet another door with a sense of finality. As if they'd finally reached their destination. "By my reckoning, this room was Wendell's private study. There's a proper office, but this is cozier. You can stay here until you're ready to face the world. You're free to use one of the bedrooms but be prepared to be cold. Even in the summer, the place never gets warm."

Relatively speaking, the study was quite modest compared to the huge great hall. But it was still bigger than the entirety of her one-bedroom apartment.

Two tall windows were on one wall, along with two equally tall bookshelves complete with a rolling ladder. Regardless of the convenient ability to reach the upper shelves, there appeared to be little order to the books crammed into every inch of space.

A scarred desk was angled in one corner with a straight-backed chair behind it, and a short Victorian sofa sat on a faded rug in the center of the room, along with an ornate coffee table and a floor lamp, which he turned on with a tug on a short chain. A fireplace surrounded by stone occupied the corner opposite the desk. It was empty and so massive that she could have stood upright inside it. But at some point, it must have seen a lot of use because the walls were blackened inside. Now there wasn't even a pile of ash.

"Do you come here regularly?" She pointed downward to emphasize that she meant this particular room. She moved closer to one of the windows and looked out. She could see his car, which helped orient her a little bit. She could also see the sunset had narrowed to a flame-bright orange licking along the horizon.

"Occasionally. I'm guessing Smitty must use it when he's around. It's usually clean enough. A lot less dusty than some of the other spaces."

She turned her attention away from the sunset. She didn't really want to know what would happen to the fireworks over the lake, did she? Had they been cancelled? Or would they be going off any minute now?

"This thing should work as long as the weather stays clear." He tapped a sturdy black rotary-dial telephone sitting on the desk before picking up the receiver. She was able to hear the dial tone from where she stood. He hung up the phone again.

"There's Wi-Fi but don't ask me what the password is. The television's from the days before it ever existed. It's never picked up more than one antenna channel. Black-and-white movies, 24/7." He nudged the portable box-shaped unit also sitting on the desk. Both phone and television looked as old-fashioned as the kitchen appliances had.

"Or I can simply reacquaint myself with some Tolkien." She plucked a very old paperback from the shelf and waved it at him.

"Or that," he agreed. "I've done it myself."

He was ready to leave her there. She could sense it even if he didn't say it.

She carefully tucked a brittle, loosened page back in line with its mates and returned the book to the same spot laying crosswise atop several others. "Thank you again for your help." After all her claims about needing time alone, she didn't want to admit a change of heart just because the castle was big and empty and seemed to have a split personality.

He found a stubby pencil in the desk drawer and scrawled a phone number on a small notepad sitting next to the television. "If you decide you need a ride, you can call me when you want to leave." He tossed the pencil back in the drawer and shut it with a snap. "I'm in town until Monday morning."

She forced a calm nod, then wanted to sink through the floor when her stomach growled loudly enough to wake whatever ghosts haunted the castle. She hadn't eaten since the scrambled egg that morning that her mama had insisted upon.

It was over that small breakfast that she'd seen the social media post.

Reeve's brows had drawn together. "I should have thought about food," he muttered. "I doubt there's anything in the kitchen cupboards."

She waved her hand at the phone. "I can call for something to be delivered from Chatelaine." Of course, she had no way to pay for it, but that was beside the point since she was lying through her teeth, anyway.

Nor was he convinced, because he pulled out his cell phone. "The only place that delivers all the way out here is Shoreline Pizza by the lake." He tapped the cracked screen a few times before handing it to her. "That's their menu. I have an account."

She raised her eyebrows and looked up at him from the phone app he'd opened.

"Everyone likes pizza," he said.

"Trey doesn't."

His gaze was steady. "I'm not Trey," he said after a beat.

She blamed her suddenly dry mouth on the second hunger pang working its way through her empty stomach.

She moistened her lips and quickly tapped in a selection of salad and a drink. "I'll pay you back for this, too." Then she mentally shrugged and added a wood-fired pepperoni pizza with extra black olives.

She didn't have to fit into a wedding dress anymore. Why not carb it up?

She submitted the order and a second later, a confirmation message appeared. Before she could even read through it, another window opened, displaying a text message.

We need to talk. Dinner next Friday?

She turned the phone so he could see the screen as she handed it back to him.

His lips twisted as he read the message and then pushed the phone into his pocket again.

She'd bet her bottom dollar that the "G" who had sent the message was a woman.

"Closest bathroom is next to the kitchen," he said. "You remember the way?"

"Of course," she lied blithely. She knew it was on the same floor, because they'd never gone up any of the staircases they'd passed. She wasn't so sure about finding which door the pizza delivery would come to, but she'd deal with that, too. "I appreciate everything, but really, I'm just ready to, uh, to be alone."

He sighed audibly. "Follow me back to the kitchen, so I know you won't get lost."

"I won't—" She broke off and ran her fingers through her hair, which launched a trio of forgotten hairpins. She picked them off the floor where they landed and joined him in the doorway.

The trip back to the kitchen was much less circuitous than she thought it would be and was aided considerably by the lights he turned on.

She also happened to periodically drop a hairpin behind her along the way and wished she hadn't forgotten her bundle of pins inside his car so she could have left even more of a trail.

The runaway bride's version of bread crumbs.

She was pretty sure Reeve didn't notice. He was too busy pointing out the powder room and then the storage room with the window and the door in which they'd entered.

"This is where the delivery guy will come." He made sure she was able to work the old bolt lock, even going so far as to step outside while she locked the stiff mechanism and then unlocked it again.

Only then did he give a final nod and leave.

She watched until he'd walked out of sight before she slowly closed the door again and leaned her forehead against it with a deep sigh. "Now what, Isabel?"

The empty room provided no answer and eventually, she straightened. Her ankle throbbed and she sat on the cold stone floor to remove her wedding sandals. She tossed them aside and rubbed her arches while she studied the engraving all around the door. The bright incandescent light shining down on the room threw the engraving into sharp relief, and when she looked at it from across the room like she was, she realized the design wasn't random at all. It was a pattern of fifty. Fifty intertwined ovals. Fifty ivy leaves. Repeating again and again, all the way up to Reeve's window.

Of all the people to help her. Reeve Fortune.

She blew out a breath and pushed to her feet. Limping slightly, she went to find her path of hairpins back to the study.

Reeve had always considered himself a practical man.

He saw a problem. He crafted a solution.

Simple.

So why did he second-guess himself every step of the way back to his car?

The mountain of fluff in his back seat was visible even in the dwindling light.

He opened his trunk, intending to transfer the gown there, but a bag of basketballs took up all the space. He'd forgotten he'd stored them a couple weeks ago as a favor for Hector, who was the guy who'd introduced Reeve to their pickup team in the first place.

He closed the trunk, bundled up the dress and carried it back to the house.

Exactly as he'd suspected, Isabel had left the side door unlocked.

It wasn't a major crime. She had a delivery coming from the pizza place. Aside from that, there was little likelihood of intruders.

He went inside, noting the discarded shoes.

He'd wondered how long she'd be able to stick it out wearing those stilts.

One of the ruffles kept popping out of his hold to tickle his nose. It was futile trying to ball it tighter. Every time he made the attempt, another ruffle popped out somewhere else.

He was silently cursing the thing when he reached the study, catching Isabel halfway up the rolling ladder.

She jumped when he entered the room, quickly wedging a book back on the shelf. Just as quickly, her gaze dropped to the bundle in his arms.

"I don't want to be caught driving around with a wedding dress in my trunk and no bride in the car," he explained. "Looks suspicious." He opened the cupboard behind the desk and began cramming it inside. The fabric was surprisingly stiff.

She descended the ladder and came to help, her hands brushing his as they conquered the task.

"Helluva dress," he said, when he finally managed to close the door on it without some portion of it sneaking back out again.

"Trey chose it."

"Then no wonder."

She was still crouched on the floor slightly below him and she gave him a look, her eyebrows lifting slightly. "No wonder what?"

Gigi often accused him of forgetting the art of tactfulness. Times like this, he had to admit she had a point.

He moved away from Isabel and leaned back against the desk. Giving her space. "No wonder the dress was so elaborate. Your fiancé likes showy things." Hell. That didn't help anything.

She'd tucked her tongue in her cheek. "After today, I'd say he's not my fiancé anymore. Thirty-two years old and starting all over again," she added under her breath.

"My sister's a couple of years older than I am and she just got engaged to be married."

"Yeah, I heard. But—" She pushed to her feet and brushed her hands together. "You're right. The gown *was* showy. Not my style at all. Talk about missing all the signs." Then she propped her hands on her slender hips and angled her head slightly. Her hair was still that messy half-up, half-down crown of curls that was as waifish as it was comical. "We could've just left the dress in one of the rooms here."

"Would've been easier," he agreed. Since he'd already convinced her of the unlikelihood of being found there, it didn't make sense to say he hadn't wanted the dress discovered in the castle any more than he wanted it discovered in his car. So he pushed away from the desk again. "I'll leave you to it."

"Do you, uh, really have to go?" she asked quickly. "I'll never be able to eat a whole pizza on my own."

He'd done as much rescuing as it was wise to do. But she was twisting her hands at her waist and her smile wasn't anywhere near as breezy as she probably hoped.

When had he become such a sucker for a vulnerable woman? Or was it just a vulnerable *Isabel*?

Either way, the answer was the same.

"Fine." Even he could hear the lack of enthusiasm in his voice. "But you're picking off all the black olives first."

Her chin lifted. "Just leaves more for me," she assured him.

He didn't know what was worse. Getting sucked in by her vulnerability, or that sudden spurt of bravado.

Despite Reeve's belief that the larder was entirely empty, they found a partially empty bag of ice in the freezer and a pouch of ground coffee that was still fragrant in the fridge, along with a can of powdered creamer and a jar of chocolate-covered almonds.

When the pizza delivery finally arrived, Isabel had concocted an iced coffee mixture that was better than decent, and by unspoken agreement, they carried everything back to the study.

Despite the olives—even though she *did* pick them off one side of the pizza—it was about as perfect a meal as Reeve could remember.

He didn't figure it was smart to dwell on the fact that it was the company versus the food that made it so.

"Is this when he built it?" Finished with her portion of pizza and salad, Isabel had been wandering around the room, the jar of almonds in her hand. She glanced at Reeve where he was sitting on the couch, his feet propped on the cocktail table. "Nineteen fifty?" She popped an almond in her mouth and pointed above the top of the window where the number fifty had been etched into the stone. "I've been noticing patterns of fifty all over the place, but right there it's actually spelled out."

"Construction was finished in the midsixties." He pulled out his cell phone when it vibrated again. His father, obviously tired of trying to reach him by phone, had switched to text messages. He sent back a swift Not now! and set the phone aside again.

He'd already responded to Gigi's earlier text message, agreeing to have dinner with her and Harrison in a week. She probably wanted to talk wedding plans or Fortune Metals business. If Harrison, who was a lawyer, had only wanted to deliver an update on his investigation into the Fortune family skeletons, he'd have just made an appointment. Even though Reeve had done what he could to make up for interfering

early on with Harrison and Gigi's budding relationship, Reeve suspected the other man hadn't entirely
forgiven him.

"I suppose it could be an indicator of Wendell's
obsession with building the castle," he told Isabel.

"The reason isn't in your great-grandfather's journal?"

"Journals," he corrected. "So far there've been fifteen. All but one hidden in the castle." And out of
the clear blue sky, his father was suddenly asking
about journals.

Isabel's faint smile was a lot more attractive to
think about than his father.

"The longest I've ever kept a diary was about two
months when I was twelve," she told him.

"What did a twelve-year-old Isabel have to write
about?"

"Her new neighbor—a thirteen-year-old boy
named Bobby with whom she might have been
slightly obsessed." She tilted the jar toward him and
when he shook his head, set it on the cocktail table.

"What happened to Bobby?"

A faint dimple in her cheek came and went. "He
taught me how to French kiss and then his family
moved to Odessa the next summer."

"Leaving you heartbroken and devastated?"

"Heartbroken but never devastated. My mother
signed me up for a summer camp that was an effec-
tive distraction."

"Where you met another Bobby?"

Her faint smile sharpened slightly. "Something like

that. Where I discovered creative writing classes."
She walked over to the rolling ladder and climbed
up several rungs. With a small push against the shelf,
the ladder—anchored by the tall horizontal rail that
spanned the wall—rolled smoothly past the window
separating one bookcase from the other. She stopped
its progress simply by grabbing another shelf.

"I played on the ladder just like that, the first time
I came here." He swirled the dregs of coffee and ice
cubes in his cut crystal glass. They'd found the glass-
ware set in the dining room. "I was ten."

"Are you saying I'm as mature as a ten-year-old
boy?"

He smiled faintly. "I'm not touching that one with
a fifty-foot pole."

When she smiled, her eyes narrowed with a slight
crinkle. It only seemed to emphasize the sparkle in
her dark brown eyes. She turned that sparkle away
from him when she faced the bookshelves again.
"There's everything here from the histories of mining to *Atlas Shrugged* to *Winnie-the-Pooh*."

"Not to mention *The Hobbit*." She'd left the
book—one of his favorites when he'd been young—
sitting crosswise atop several other fantasies. As old
as the titles were, Reeve assumed they'd belonged
to Wendell.

"How much time do you spend here?" Isabel asked.
"You said it'd been years since you were here last."

He shrugged. "I come here occasionally." Usually when he most needed Walter's advice. Reeve

had learned more from reading his great-grandfather's writings after his death than he ever had from his own father in real life. For some reason, though, Reeve had never taken the journals out of the castle. As if doing so disturbed their final resting place. Weird, considering the one that had been left at Fortune Metals was sitting right now on his nightstand at his place in Aransas Pass.

He set aside his glass—which really deserved a fine whiskey versus the watery coffee it contained—and pushed to his feet. He joined her in front of the bookcase and freed a thin volume from one of the lower shelves.

He showed her the embossed date on the front of the leather cover below Walter's monogram. "Nineteen thirty-six. That's the year Walter Fortune became a father. He was twenty-four. He and his wife, Effie, had been married a year, and he'd already doubled the size of Fortune Mining. It's the earliest year I've found, but I'd lay odds he journaled throughout his entire life."

He flipped open the cover and looked at the pages within. Covered with Walter's handwriting; sometimes rushed, but always deliberate. Always thoughtful. Walter's writing was as familiar as Reeve's own.

"He had his own home," he told Isabel. "Always had. First in Chatelaine not far from the original mining office. Then later, the much larger one at the point on Lake Chatelaine."

"The only thing on the point of the lake is the LC Club."

"He deeded his home to Chatelaine after his death. That was more than twenty years ago. Now it's the LC Club."

She looked stunned. "I didn't know that."

"Most people don't. Only one part of the building is original to their house. The rest of it—particularly the lakeside portion with all the balconies and terraces—has been built since." He stopped short of offering to show her sometime. "Walter chose to store his journals here, in his brother's abandoned castle."

"Why here, though? Oh. Silly. Because he'd given away his home to the town."

He shook his head. "I don't think so." He lifted the journal. "The only time I saw him actually with one of his journals—*this* one—was the one time he brought me here." He touched the ladder. "I played on this very ladder, and he made a point of me seeing him shelve the journal right here among these books. Walter never did anything without deliberation. He *wanted* me to know it was here. Then he died. I didn't come back until I was a lot older. Before long, I discovered there was more than that one volume. A journal for each year." Filled from front to back with Walter's thoughts on everything from the best way to tamp the tobacco in his pipe to the best way to conquer business adversaries.

"How old was he when he died?"

"Eighty-eight, but he journaled practically up to the end." Half the pages of that last volume were sadly empty. "We discovered his last one in a bunch of business papers at his office in Corpus Christi a

few years ago. We were working on an archival project for our mining museum." When Reeve realized
it was Walter's final journal, he'd put it on his nightstand where it had sat for two full years.

He'd only picked it up again a month ago.

Isabel was giving him a surprised look. "Fortune
Metals has a mining museum?

"It's part of an educational thing. We fund it, but
the project is managed by another foundation."

"Fortune Metals and education. Who'd have
thought?"

He shrugged. "Our history goes back a long way.
There's an exhibit at the museum in Chatelaine chronicling our company's role in the town's development,
too."

"Guess I'll have to go there and read all about it,"
she said lightly. "So, if the earliest journal is from
1936 and you've only found fifteen, that leaves a lot
of years unaccounted for between the first one and
the last one. How do you know it wasn't just something he did sporadically?"

"Because he said so himself. He wrote because he
didn't have anyone with whom he could completely
share his thoughts. He was particularly protective of
shielding his wife from the day-to-day messiness of
business. He was close to Wendell, but he was also
twenty-five years older than him. They were half-
brothers. Different moms. Everyone needs a sounding board and I think Walter's was in the pages that
he wrote." He saw a distant flash of lightning through

the window between the bookcases. "The rest of the years exist. Somewhere. Here in the castle. Or buried in packing boxes at Fortune Metals like the last one was."

He just hadn't found them yet. Gigi didn't even know about them, and she'd been Walter's shadow.

And now it turned out that PJ *did* know. And for some reason yet to be explained, he was nagging Reeve to find one of those missing years.

He worked the journal back into its usual spot. He had enough on his plate without worrying about PJ's latest scheme.

"My great-grandmother died in 1965 of cancer," he told Isabel. "She was only fifty. Personally, I think that's the significance behind that." He pointed at the number atop the window casing. "Wendell was about the same age as Walter and Effie's son. She did more raising of Wendell than his own mother did." Just as the housekeepers had been more influential on Gigi and Reeve than Delphine Fortune. "I think losing Effie was as devastating to Wendell as it was to Walter. He left Texas shortly after she died and never returned." It was only Reeve's supposition, but the timeline fit.

"Maybe he had a broken heart from an entirely different relationship," Isabel countered. "A romance of his own."

He shrugged. "Maybe. I only know what—"

"—your great-grandfather wrote," she finished.

A faint rumble of thunder followed another flash of lighting.

Two rungs up from the floor, she was nearly eye level to Reeve, and the smile had disappeared from her eyes and a vertical line had formed between her smooth dark eyebrows. "You telling me all this... You really *don't* know who I am. Do you."

It wasn't a question. He answered anyway. "You're a woman with the good sense to avoid marriage."

She frowned. "I wasn't avoiding marriage. Just marriage to Trey."

Splitting hairs as far as he was concerned. It had taken his sister years to recover from her failed marriage to a cheat. Eventually, she'd focused her considerable attention on becoming a life coach and then she'd met Harrison when Reeve had gone outside of his usual legal teams and hired the attorney to deal with the Mariana Sanchez situation.

Isabel's teeth caught her soft, rosy lip and she climbed down from the ladder. She tugged the hem of her T-shirt and seemed to pull back her shoulders, as if she was bracing herself. "I appreciate everything you've done today. And hearing about your family is very interesting. But there's something you really need to know before you say anything else."

That she wasn't over Trey just because she didn't go through with the wedding?

"If it's about Trey—"

She cut him off. "I write—" She jumped when the window next to her flashed with white light and thunder clapped, loud and sharp. "It wasn't supposed to rain tonight."

"You write..." he prompted, thinking about the way

she'd reverently handled the old fiction novels on the shelves.

She moistened her lips. "I... I'm the one who writes *The Chatelaine Report*."

Chapter Six

Right on cue, the electricity flickered and thunder boomed, but Isabel's admission still seemed louder.

She'd *needed* to tell Reeve the truth. He would never have spoken so freely about his family if he'd known she authored the blog he'd threatened to sue.

She held her breath, waiting while the lamp flickered again. Despite the storm outside, the electricity held up, though. Well enough for her to watch his brilliant blue eyes change hues like water icing over.

"*You* wrote that garbage? About that food truck woman?"

No matter how prepared she thought she was, her nerves bristled defensively. On any other day, she might have been able to exercise more control. Especially when he'd gone out of his way to help her in such spectacularly unexpected fashion.

But it had been a terrible day.

And the way he was looking at her stung. As if she'd suddenly become something he ought to scrape off the bottom of his shoe.

All because she'd written one blog post about Mariana Sanchez's effort to connect to her own flesh and blood.

She willed herself not to jump when it thundered again. "If you had one iota of actual interest in the small businesses you gobble up with FortuneMedia, you wouldn't have to ask the question." If Reeve had ever read any of her other blog entries, he'd have known that for months she'd been writing about the effects of Wendell's bequests to his grandchildren. All but one of whom lived right in Chatelaine.

It was only when the story directly affected *Reeve* that he'd cared.

She pointed at him. "Not to mention the fact that you could have just responded to my request for a comment without siccing your attorneys on me. And by the way—" her voice rose "—that *food truck woman* has a name!"

"Mariana Sanchez," he said deliberately, "is no more Walter's granddaughter than you are. She's just another interloper trying to worm her way into the family's bank account."

"Did you learn that cynicism from Walter?" She tsked. "I feel sorry for you."

"Save your sympathy. I've spent my entire adult life fighting to keep Walter's legacy intact. One easily disproven claim from some woman from Rambling

Rose is nothing in comparison to some. You should have checked your facts better before you reported them in that blog of yours."

"All I *did* was talk about the facts! Mariana San-chez has DNA tests that prove she's a Fortune. That is a fact, whether *you* like it or not. And for months, you and your sister had been ignoring her request to meet!"

His expression tightened. "Therefore, she takes her story to a *blog*?"

"There's nothing wrong with blogs," she said hotly. "FortuneMedia is involved in publishing them from Texas to Timbuktu! Or is that what you do? Buy 'em up so you can just close 'em down when they say something you don't like?"

He pushed his fingers through his hair as if he wanted to yank it out. "You're worse than Gigi. I'm not closing anything down any more than I'm tearing buildings down!" He dropped his hands to his hips and bowed his head, clearly working to regain his temper.

She wasn't finished, though. "Considering how many Fortunes there are around Texas—and a lot of them have been gossiped about way more than *you*— it's a wonder there's a free press left at all! And just so you know, Mariana *didn't* come to me. I heard about her from another source and reached out to her to get the real story. That food truck you sneer at is at the center of a town where she's beloved." Rambling Rose was several hours away from Chatelaine and a great deal more developed. "She's a business owner and a chef and you can believe me when I say there

are plenty of other *Fortunes* who don't look down
their nose at her! All Mariana Sanchez wants is to be
acknowledged. To understand where she fits on the
mighty Fortune tree. Is that so wrong?"

He raised his head. His eyes were still chilly, but
his voice was even. "She doesn't fit on *this* branch.
My great-grandfather valued family more than anything else. Including the business that was his entire
life's work. If he'd had some—" he waved a dismis-
sive hand "—fling that ended up producing another
child, he would have acknowledged it. Period."

"You could have just said that was your comment
instead of calling your lawyers!" She realized her
cheeks were wet. Horrified, she turned her back on
him and snatched up one of the paper napkins left
over from their pizza.

If she'd had somewhere to go, she'd have gone.

But she'd already done as much running for the
day as she was evidently capable of doing, because
all she did was plop down on the sofa. The lamp beside her flickered again.

He muttered an oath. "Don't cry."

A helpful comment if there ever was one.

She glared at him, even though she could feel another tear burning down her cheek. "I'm not crying
because of you," she assured thickly. "I never cry."

He sighed deeply. Audibly.

Any minute now, she figured he'd tell her to call
a cab. Get the heck out of his family's oddball castle.

And by the way, don't bother coming to work on
Monday, either.

She swiped her nose with the napkin and pushed to her feet. Her knees felt shaky, but she gave him a wide berth as she circled him to get to the desk. She picked up the phone to call her parents and stuck her finger in the rotary dial and dragged it around. Then the next number. The third. It took forever and when she reached the fourth number, she swore, because it wasn't even right. She was too used to the ease of cell phones and this archaic instrument of frustration had been designed by a lunatic.

Reeve tugged the receiver out of her hand and set his cell phone in its place. "Use this," he said quietly.

Her shoulders shook with a jagged breath, and when she did nothing with his phone but allow it to slide back onto the desk, she felt his arms come around her shoulders. "I didn't intend to upset you," he murmured. "Everything will be all right."

"How?" She wanted his comfort like she wanted a hole in her head. But his wide chest felt strong and warm beneath her cheek and instead of pushing him away, her fingers twisted into his shirt, and she cried harder.

She, who hadn't cried since she was a little girl.

"It just will." Reeve's voice was deep and soft.

She wished she could believe it.

Eventually, even the tears of a runaway bride who never cried had to run out.

Reeve settled her on the sofa, and she immediately closed her eyes, curling into an exhausted ball. After a few minutes, he knew she'd fallen asleep.

There was no way she'd deliberately fake that occasional soft little snore.

He plucked a woven throw from the basket next to the fireplace and carefully spread it over her slight form.

She didn't stir.

He'd wait an hour, he told himself. If she was still sleeping, he'd leave.

And if she wakens? Then what?

He ignored the voice in his head and gathered up the trash from their supper and went back to the kitchen.

The electric coffeepot they'd used earlier was still sitting on the center of the stove and he rinsed out the dregs and got it ready to brew another pot, though he didn't plug it in.

Right now, coffee was the last thing he was interested in drinking.

A little hunting under the sheets in the dining room scored a crystal decanter filled with something that smelled promising and he poured a finger in a fresh glass.

The scotch was strong enough to melt hair off a wildebeest. It'd do.

He returned to the study and sat in the uncomfortable chair behind the desk. The lightning show was still going on outside the windows, and he pulled out his cell phone. It was five in the morning in Paris. Way too early for the hours that he knew his parents typically kept.

In his mind, he replayed PJ's conversation. *Walter*

kept a journal once. Before he served in the war. My
father once mentioned reading it, so I doubt it was
ever destroyed. You can remember what Walter was
like. He kept every record there ever was. I need you
to find the journal and send it to me.

The existence of a journal was unquestionable.
Equally unquestionable was that Reeve wasn't going
to hand it over to PJ just because he asked. His father rarely did anything that wasn't self-serving first.

But Reeve *did* wonder why PJ thought it was a onetime thing. It was as odd as Gigi never knowing about
them, either. Maybe Philip Sr. had known. He'd been
Walter's successor at the helm of Fortune Metals for less
than ten years before dying when he'd been just forty
years old. PJ had been a teenager. Too young to take
over the company, and Walter had taken on the mantle
yet again until his grandson had been old enough. But
even after that point, he'd kept an office at Fortune Metals that he'd visited nearly every day until he'd suffered
a debilitating stroke shortly before he died.

After that, PJ had been left to run Fortune Metals
solo. But before long, he'd tired of the responsibility
and he and Delphine moved back to her native France
and Fortune Metals landed in Reeve's lap. More correctly, what landed in Reeve's lap was a company that
bore little resemblance to what he'd expected since PJ
had secretly sold off nearly half the stock to Dwyer
Tusker, one of the members on the board of directors.

It had taken Reeve years to regain control of that
stock, years of fighting Tusker and his cronies who'd
wanted to parse out Fortune Metals until there was

nothing left but profit in their pockets, but it had not been easy. And it had taken a long damn time. Time when his attention couldn't stay focused on FortuneMedia, which he'd founded before he'd ever been saddled with the mess that his father had made.

Unlike Fortune Metals—which had grown over generations from a simple mining operation into a billion-dollar conglomerate that Walter headquartered in Corpus Christi—FortuneMedia was all Reeve's.

It had been his money that had started it. His sweat. His time.

And once he'd wrested back control of Fortune Metals, he'd begun turning FortuneMedia into the successful communications company that it was now. Yeah, he had people to help run it. But he still prided himself on keeping his hand involved in more personal ways than he could ever do with Fortune Metals. Which was why he'd decided to use one of the offices in that quaint old house leased by Stellar Productions as a convenient base for FortuneMedia.

And why not when the building was already owned by the Fortune Trust?

His family had an allegiance to its history in Chatelaine no matter how much they'd grown.

Even PJ had thought so. To a degree. When he'd played at being the CEO of Fortune Metals, he hadn't entirely closed down their local presence, keeping the small satellite office near the lake.

That satellite office was still operating, run by a long-time tight staff. And Reeve spent a lot of hours there. But the Stellar Productions building some ten miles away gave him another taste of…starting out. Of challenge.

Tastes that had started to fade lately.

Even if Gigi had just about gone bananas when she'd learned his plans.

She'd gotten over it mostly, but that was owed more to what Reeve considered "the Harrison effect" than by anything Reeve had personally done, including adding Gigi to the Fortune Metals board of directors.

A crack of thunder made the windows rattle and he set aside his unfinished drink. He looked out to see if it was raining, but as far as he could tell, it was just a noisy light show.

Isabel had twisted around, and the woven throw was barely hanging on, but the dry storm hadn't wakened her.

He'd never slept on the sofa. Too short for him, for one thing. But it also wasn't particularly comfortable, with cushions that had gone lumpy over the decades.

He could chance moving her to one of the bedrooms upstairs or leave her where she was.

His fingers curled. It wasn't his business if she was comfortable or not. He'd done what his conscience demanded earlier that day when she'd plowed into him on the church steps.

How had he not known she wrote that damn blog?

Why hadn't Gigi ever mentioned it? His sister was associated with Stellar Productions, too. It produced her podcast, *Gigi's Journey*.

But then why *would* Gigi have specifically mentioned Isabel?

It wasn't as if they were one big social group. As far as he'd known, Gigi only went to Chatelaine to record episodes of her podcast. She'd spend the night— never at his place by the lake, though, because that would have been like admitting they were relatives— and head back to Corpus Christi. They'd often gone months without ever crossing each other's paths.

There'd been a time when they'd been closer. When she was just his big sis and the only one who'd take the time to sit and read stories with him. She'd even been the one to convince him that golf wasn't an exercise in stupidity, and they'd spent hours together on the greens.

But those years had passed.

She'd been the trust fund baby, adored and doted on by Walter. Then she'd gotten married right out of high school, and he'd learned the only one he could count on was himself. Only in the last month had Gigi shared *her* side of the story—how she'd always believed that Walter wanted *her* to run Fortune Metals and how betrayed she'd felt that the company had ultimately been handed to Reeve.

There was nothing that Reeve could do to change the past. He knew what Walter had really expected, no matter how Gigi remembered things. But in the end, he'd been as guilty of being content with the status quo as his sister had been.

And yet…thanks to the Sanchez woman's claim, they'd seen more of each other in the last month than they had in years. And Reeve had been forced to acknowledge that he'd been as judgmental about Gigi's role in their family as she'd been about him.

Not even Grampy thought he could control the entire world, Reeve. Why do you?

He pulled the blanket back up over Isabel's shoulders, then went to the desk. He pulled off another sheet from the pad next to the phone and wrote out a note that he left on the cocktail table where Isabel would be sure to see it when she awoke.

I'm sorry.

Then he went back to the kitchen and gathered up the trash from their dinner and carried it all out to his car. As many times as he'd prowled around the castle, he had no idea where the trash can was currently located or even if there was one.

He'd dispose of it all when he got back to town.

He couldn't lock the door from the outside, which meant locking it from the inside and climbing back out the window. He managed it, but it wasn't as easy from the inside where the climb had fewer hand- and footholds.

He needed to just get a key to the place. The caretaker would have the masters.

Otherwise, he'd better kick up his rock-climbing workouts. He was pretty sure his basketball night was going to become free just as soon as Trey discovered Reeve's involvement in the flight of his fiancée.

Then, with one last glance at the sleeping castle, he got in his car and drove home.

* * *

The aroma of fresh coffee woke Isabel.

She squinted at the bright light shining through the tall windows and groaned as she untangled herself from a plaid blanket.

Reeve had covered her up.

She swung her legs down and rotated her ankle. That pain was gone. But she had a brand-new one thanks to the kink in her neck. She rubbed it for a while, studying the room around her.

The paper plates and boxes from the night before were gone from the cocktail table and it had been wiped clean.

Her wedding shoes sat neatly on the floor next to it.

Something else Reeve had to have done. Because she'd left them sitting in that empty storage room.

She pushed off the lumpy couch and stretched. Then she picked up the phone on the desk to call Ronnie, but the phone was noticeably silent.

No dial tone. She hung up again and went over to the window. The blue sky looked like it had been washed clean and was being dried by white puffballs. It must have rained.

She turned from the sight and followed the scent of coffee to the kitchen.

Reeve was sitting at the table reading a newspaper. The pants and lipstick-stained dress shirt from the night before were gone. In their place was a pale gray T-shirt that hugged his torso and a pair of jeans that were surprisingly ragged.

She didn't know why she found the sight arresting. She'd seen him play ball with Trey and his friends more than a few times. He certainly hadn't worn a three-piece suit and tie while doing so.

Even more striking, though, were his dark-rimmed eyeglasses when he looked her way as she aimed straight for the coffeepot and the empty cup and saucer that sat on the counter next to it, along with a little carton of cream. The real kind.

"Good morning," he greeted. His eyes looked particularly blue through the glasses.

She focused on pouring the coffee. She had a headache and a literal pain in her neck, and undoubtedly looked just as bad as she felt, while *he* looked like an advertisement for…anything that needed a seriously good-looking man to sell it.

She blinked a few times and realized part of her problem seeing clearly was the little strip of false eyelashes that was coming loose. "Morning," she mumbled a little belatedly. She pulled at the lash, and it came away with a painful little tug that probably pulled a few of her real lashes with it.

"Breakfast's inside the oven." His words were accompanied by the soft snap of his newspaper. "Didn't know what you'd want so I brought a couple different things. They might still be warm. I didn't think you'd sleep this long."

She surreptitiously felt her other eyelid as she leaned down to pull open the oven door and look inside.

A half dozen takeout containers sat on the top rack.

"I didn't expect you to bring anything. Thank you."
She finally found the second eyelash strip sticking
to her cheek.

Heaven help her.

She closed the oven door without taking anything
out and sidled toward the doorway. "I'm just, uh,
going to—" She pushed open the squeaky door and
escaped through it.

If he was laughing, at least she couldn't hear it over
that horrendously squeaky hinge.

Her reflection in the powder room mirror was even
more horrifying than she'd feared.

She washed her hands and then scrubbed her face
with cold water and soap from the value-sized dispenser of GreatStore liquid soap sitting on the edge
of the sink.

Then she used her fingers to try to restore some
sense to her hair. But too many hair products, too
many hairpins and too little attention to it the night
before had left it entirely unrestorable.

She finally gave up.

Despite the soap dispenser, there weren't any towels and since the front of her shirt was already damp
from the water she'd splashed around, she pulled it off
completely and wet a little edge of the hem and used
it to wipe her teeth. It wasn't exactly perfect, but at
least when she was done, her mouth didn't feel woolly.

She shook out the T-shirt and pulled it back on.
She was grateful that it was as loose as it was. The
bathroom was already cold enough without adding
a damp shirt on top of things.

She still plucked it away from her breasts before going back through that noisy swinging door.

Reeve didn't even glance up at her from the newspaper.

Small mercies.

She topped off the coffee cup and drizzled cream into it before pulling the plastic containers out of the oven. He hadn't turned on any heat—the containers would have probably melted—but the contents were still warm.

Her stomach growled hollowly before she could even taste the first slice of bacon. It wasn't quite as crispy as she preferred, but it still tasted heavenly. Standing right there at the counter, she finished it greedily. Then she carried the small feast over to the table and sat down across from Reeve. "Where'd you get all the food?"

He glanced at her over the rims of his eyeglasses as he took a sip of coffee from a cup identical to the one that he'd set out for her. In his large hand, the delicate cup looked like it came from a child's tea set. "The Chef's Table at the LC Club."

She winced a little. The Chef's Table had been the primary caterer for the wedding reception-that-wasn't.

Reeve didn't seem to notice her reaction as he continued. "They always serve brunch on Sundays."

"Brunch!" She stopped wondering what had been done with all that food. "What time is it?"

He looked like he was trying not to smile as he focused on his newspaper again. "Nearly noon."

She wanted to lay her head facedown on the table. "I really should call my family."

In answer, he slid a cell phone across the table to her. It was different from the one from the day before. No cracked screen for one thing. And no FortuneMedia logo on the screen saver. "You replaced your phone already?"

"I have efficient assistants, all headed up by a dragon named Cora. Go ahead. Feel free. Or use the Methuselah in the study if you want some privacy."

"It's dead." And what did privacy matter when he knew the truth about her now?

She dialed Ronnie first.

Her sister answered on the second ring, sounding breathless. "This better be you, Isabel, and not another spam caller trying to sell me new windows."

"It's me."

"Where are you?"

"Lake Chatelaine." It was close enough to accurate since Isabel didn't know precisely where the castle was located.

"With *Trey*?" Ronnie's voice went up an octave.

"No! I'm not with Trey."

"Thank God for that," her sister muttered.

"What, um, what happened after I—"

"—pulled the vanishing act? Trey told everyone that you'd taken ill. *Taken ill*," Ronnie repeated scoffingly. "Like the wedding is just postponed until you're better."

The pain behind Isabel's eyebrows deepened.

"Mom and Dad are fine, by the way. Relieved if

you ask me, though Blake and I had to get home to the kids last night, so we didn't have a lot of time to talk."

"I'll call them soon. What about Paige?"

Ronnie laughed a little. "She and Auntie Pearl were going around collecting the flower petals from the aisle thinking they'll try freezing them to use at Paige's wedding."

Isabel smiled at the image of that. Their younger sister, Paige, was engaged to her high school sweetheart, and they were planning to marry as soon as they finished college. And as tight a budget as they had, she looked for any way to save money. In that way, she was as frugal as their father's older sister, Pearl. "Someone might as well get something out of it," she said.

"Don't suppose you've talked to him." Ronnie's tone sobered.

Isabel sighed. "Not yet."

"Do you still have your apartment key hidden in that plant under the window?"

"Yes."

"Blake and I will take your bed back today."

"I gave it to Sasha, though."

"She's six years old. She'll be fine with her old one. It's still in the garage."

"Are you sure?"

"Positive. How long do you plan to hide out?"

"I don't know." She sneaked a look at Reeve through her lashes. They didn't do as good a job of shielding as the fake ones. He was looking right back at her and her face got hot when their gazes connected. She folded a piece of bacon and jammed it into her mouth. "Probably not much longer," she said around it. "I'll let you know."

"Y'better," Ronnie said, and hung up.

Isabel set the cell phone on the table and slid it back toward Reeve. "Thank you."

"Trey was in the restaurant this morning, too," he said.

"Did you talk to him?" She didn't really want to know, but she also couldn't stop herself from asking.

"He didn't even notice me. Trace and Rebecca were there." He named Trey's parents. "Plus a few others that I didn't recognize."

She knew that a good portion of the out-of-towners had planned to stay overnight at the hotel adjacent to the LC Club. If she'd been more involved with the details of her own wedding, she'd have been able to say exactly who and how many.

But those were details left to the coordinator.

"Do you suppose *undoing* all the details of this aborted wedding can be left to the wedding coordinator that Trey insisted on hiring? Probably not." She answered her own question. "I made this mess. It'll be up to me to clean it up."

"I'm no expert, but it seems to me that Trey is the one who made the mess."

She wasn't sure what it said about her that her appetite wasn't diminished at all. She opened another one of the containers and found two slices of French toast complete with a miniature bottle of maple syrup.

She twisted off the cap and emptied the entire thing, leaving the toast swimming in syrup. She sawed at the soaked concoction with the edge of a plastic fork. "You've never been married?"

Reeve shook his head.

"Ever been close?"

He shook his head again and slowly turned to another page in the newspaper. "Never been interested."

"In women?"

That did earn a look. An amused one. "None who was important enough to make me want to take a day off work. I don't do relationships."

Shocker. "But if you did, that's the end-all be-all indicator? If you take off work, it means she's marriage material?"

His lips tilted even more as he focused on his newspaper again. "It was for Walter."

She propped her elbows on the table and studied him. "He was a big influence on you."

"Still is." He finally closed the paper, folded it in half and set it aside. Then he got up and refilled both of their coffee cups. Instead of sitting again, though, he leaned back against the counter and crossed one foot over the other before sipping from the dinky cup. With his thick straight hair brushed carelessly over his brow and the dusty boots on his feet, he looked more cowboy than tycoon. "What're your plans for today?"

"Aside from hiding out from everyone I know, including Trey? I don't know. What're your plans for today?"

"Same."

"You're hiding out from a girl who cheated on you?"

He smiled slightly. "There's a girl," he allowed. "But not the way you think."

"Well," she drawled, "I think we've established that she's not someone you're considering marrying."

"Pretty safe conclusion."

"A family member then? Don't worry. You can tell me. It's not like I'll dare mention it in *The Chatelaine Report*."

He pulled off his glasses and set them on the counter. "I never intended to actually go through with legal action."

"Then why threaten it?"

"Sometimes carrying the big stick sufficiently accomplishes the task." He straightened abruptly and set aside the cup. "Want to go for a walk? I found some rubber boots earlier that you can wear."

She blinked slightly. "Um. Okay. But I'd kill for a shower first. Do you know if there are any towels in this tiny little shack?"

"Probably. If there aren't, I've got an extra in my gym bag in the car." He waited a beat, as if reading her expression. "Don't worry. I just picked it up from the laundry. Perfectly clean and fresh."

The idea of using *his* towel at all had disturbed her. Not whether it was clean or not.

But all she did was shake her head at him. "You send your towels *out* to be laundered?"

He shrugged. "How else are they going to get clean?"

She just rolled her eyes and laughed. "You Fortunes really do live in a different world."

Chapter Seven

The castle *did* have bath towels.

They found them in an armoire at the end of a long hall on the third floor.

"Why they're all the way up here," Reeve said, "is just one more mystery."

The towels had smelled exactly like they'd been shut away for the last fifty years, but they weren't moth-eaten, so that said something about the effectiveness of the cedar lining inside the armoire.

She wasn't so lucky in finding shampoo or soap and if she didn't want to waste even more time looking, or resort to using the dispenser of hand soap from the powder room, she had to accept the offer of Reeve's shower gel from his gym bag.

Which was why the lavish bathroom she chose on

the second floor smelled like Reeve when she left it again a regrettably fast twenty minutes later.

She didn't want to dwell on the fact that *she* smelled like him, too. Or that she could have spent an hour lolling about in the hammered copper bathtub that was big enough to swim in.

Most importantly, she didn't want to think about the fact that she'd even paid *attention* to the way he smelled.

Great, a voice whispered inside her head. *Reeve smells great.*

She told the voice to shut its trap and went downstairs again, where she found him in the study. There was a big cardboard box on the coffee table, and he was methodically pulling books out of it.

"I don't think any more books are going to fit on the shelves."

He glanced her way. "You're right about that." He hadn't put on his glasses again and she wondered if he wore contact lenses. Maybe they were the reason his eyes were so unbelievably blue. "These were in the storage shed where I found the boots." He tilted his head toward the pair of dark green rubber boots sitting next to the doorway. "Thought you might need some socks, though."

She barely caught the small bundle he suddenly tossed her way. She unwound the two pristine white sport socks. She didn't bother asking if he'd found them somewhere in the castle. Not when they had the Fortune Metals logo printed on them.

She perched on the sofa, as far away from him

as she could get—which wasn't far considering the shortness of cushion and the broadness of shoulder. "Your company issues its own socks?" She pulled on the first one rapidly, not giving herself any time to think about it.

"Have a whole catalog of swag." He sounded disinterested as he continued pulling out books and stacking them next to the box. He'd glance at the cover and set it aside. "And an entire department of employees who handle it."

Fortune Metals was one of the largest employers in Texas. She could only imagine how many departments and how many employees there were.

She pulled on the second sock. They were too long; the heel reached up to her ankle, but they felt welcoming all the same. Warm and soft against the chilliness of the castle interior. She reached for the rubber boots. One glance was enough to tell her they'd be too big.

He pulled out a stack of disorderly photographs and old postcards and tossed them next to the books he'd stacked, and some of them slid off the table onto the floor.

"Looking for something in particular?"

"No." He didn't say anything more, but she knew he was lying.

She leaned over to pick up the photos, carefully straightening them. "Was this Wendell?" She turned the top photo of a lanky man with a pensive expression toward him.

He glanced at it and shook his head. "My grandfather, Philip." His fingers brushed hers as he took the stack of photos and thumbed through them. "That's Wendell." He flipped the black and white photo out of the stack like a card dealer.

She picked it up and studied it for a moment, taking in the shock of hair falling across Wendell's forehead and a familiar, sharp-edged jaw that also belonged to the man sitting beside her. She squared the edges of the stack again and set it carefully on the coffee table. Then she stood and pushed her feet into the boots. They reached halfway to her knees, and they felt very rubbery against her bare calves.

She walked back to the doorway and the soles scuffed along the floor no matter how much she picked up her feet. She'd tied the hem of her wrinkled pink T-shirt in a knot near her hip and with the black leggings and rubber boots, she felt quite a sight.

It was still better than being Mrs. Trey Fitzgerald.

The wardrobe for her first outing as his new wife had involved three different outfits; she'd planned for multiple options since Trey had kept their honeymoon destination a secret.

He'd said he wanted to surprise her.

She guessed she'd beaten him to that particular punch.

She propped her hands on her hips. "So, Mr. Fortune. Are we going for a walk or not?"

"Don't call me that."

"It's your name."

"Reeve is my name."

"So?"

"You've never used it."

She pressed her lips together for a moment. "All right, *Reeve*—" saying his name felt more momentous than it should have "—where are we headed?"

He tossed another handful of photographs and faded postcards onto the others and rose. "Wherever you want. The formal garden went wild a long time ago."

"As long as I don't have to climb through a window to get there, I don't care."

He smiled slightly and led the way back through the winding halls to the side door. Her boots scraped and thumped the entire way.

He pulled open the door and she stepped out into the warm, welcome sunshine.

"Ahh," she exhaled, tilting her wet head back a little and closing her eyes against the sunlight. "So good."

Reeve made a grunting sound that might have been agreement. She opened her eyes again when she felt him brush past her and she followed him along the sidewalk.

He didn't head for the front of the castle, but the rear, walking around another wing where the moat of bushes angled sharply downward, following the line of steps cut into the hill. She was glad for the iron railing as they went down them. Some were still wet.

"That's the shed where I found the boots," he told her when they reached the grassy ground level again and gestured toward a single-story building with two windows flanking an open door.

It looked a lot larger than a "shed" to her, but she

supposed it was all a matter of perspective. Her parents were comfortably well off, but they'd never sent out their towels to be laundered. They'd assigned that chore to their three daughters. Just as they'd assigned chores like mowing the grass every weekend and washing the windows every spring.

She took a skip to catch up with Reeve and nearly pulled her foot right out of its boot. She tugged it back on as she hurried along. "What happened to your uncle Wendell, anyway? After he left the United States once Effie died."

"He traveled a lot and then died, too." Reeve squinted slightly against the sunlight as they passed a bronze statue of a woman holding out a silver orb. "That's the last piece of art he commissioned but it wasn't finished until after he died. Walter was the only one of his brothers to live a long life. None of his siblings from his father's second marriage were as lucky."

She wasn't sure what had prompted Reeve's loquaciousness, particularly when he knew the truth about her. "How many more brothers did Walter have besides Wendell?"

"Two." He looked like he'd swallowed something bitter. "Elias and Edgar," he added. "They apparently died as young men, too."

"No sisters?"

He shook his head. "Wendell was the youngest." He continued walking.

She tugged up her boots again, deciding it would

be wise to ignore the *far as I know* that he'd added under his breath. "How many acres are here?"

"A little over seventy. Not that many, when you think about it."

She gave him a look. "Seventy acres seems like a lot to me."

"It's less area than the block where the Stellar office is," he commented. "My great-grandfather bought that block and everything on it, plus the two on either side before I was born."

She blinked a little. "You mean you already owned the building before you bought Stellar Productions? I thought Diana Dawson owned the building. What about the other businesses down there?" Another thought hit her, and she gave him a quick look. "What about my apartment building?"

"*I* don't own Stellar's building or any of the others. The Fortune Trust does. And I already said I didn't realize there was an apartment building."

She narrowed her eyes, studying his profile. "Who controls the trust?"

He slid a glance her way and she huffed out a choked snort. "*You* do." She answered her own question.

He just lifted his hands, his expression impassive. "Buck has to stop somewhere."

"Is there anything you *don't* control?"

It was his turn to offer a soft snort. But what that was supposed to mean was anyone's guess, because he didn't elaborate.

They passed a couple more statues—one that was

marble, another in bronze—and both were of women. Slender-figured, delicate women. Wendell had a type, she decided silently.

Eventually, they reached a long, narrow pond shaded on side by massive cottonwoods. Yet another statue lurked in the shadows. A woman kneeling as if reaching toward the water.

Reeve aimed for the weathered bench that was positioned near the statue and they both sat.

Isabel stretched out her legs and looked at the water beyond the toes of her dark green boots. Twenty-four hours earlier, she'd been sitting in a chair having fake eyelashes glued in place and her hair wound into its complicated style.

So why was she so acutely aware of Reeve sitting beside her? Was it just because he was so different from Trey?

Something was wrong with her, that's why. The last thing she needed was to rebound from one disaster to another.

Yet when Reeve suddenly stretched, she almost expected him to put his arm around her.

But all he did was stand again and walk over to the water's edge where he crouched and scooped up a handful of water to sluice over the back of his neck. "Hotter than I realized."

She pressed her tongue against the roof of her mouth for a moment. "Yeah." It sounded as strangled as it felt. She looked away from the play of muscles beneath his gray shirt to the statue. "I've noticed that Wendell only seems to have statues of women."

"Statues of Effie, if you ask me. He was closer to her than his own mother."

Or statues of the woman who had borne his child, leading to the passel of Maloney grandchildren. She kept the thought to herself, not wanting to rock the peaceable moment. "Were Edgar and Elias as close to her as Wendell?"

"No idea. The only mention of them at all is in Walter's final journal, so I assume they weren't close. There are too many gaps of time between journals to be certain." He cupped his hand into the pond again. He ran his hand around his neck once more, and then through his hair.

Isabel got up and walked around the statue and down to the water's edge as well. Despite the shade, the water was surprisingly clear. More blue than green. She could see the pebbles on the bottom and a swarm of little tadpoles darting around them. She didn't particularly consider herself squeamish about tadpoles, but she dunked her fingers into the water only up to her knuckles, well away from the depths.

Even the inch of surface water was cool, though. She smoothed her wet fingers down her throat and sighed slightly, her gaze wandering from the thick trees on one side to the other where only scrubby brush clung to the bank. "It's a pretty spot here."

"Yeah." He straightened and flicked his hand. Water droplets flew out, catching the dappled light before rejoining the softly rippling pond surface.

For some reason, Isabel looked down at her engagement ring. Out of pure habit, she pushed at the big diamond with her thumb, centering it. It, too, glinted in the sunlight.

"All you have to do is call him."

Startled, she looked up at Reeve. "Trey?"

"If you're having second thoughts."

"Is that part of the rescue-the-runaway-bride rules? Provide counsel and return livery service when required?" She didn't look at him. "Do *you* think I should be having second thoughts? Go back and beg pardon from a man who doesn't know how to keep his tongue out of other women's mouths?"

"It doesn't matter what I think. But I doubt you'd have to beg. The guy always seemed pretty crazy about you."

"Crazy about me, but tells his friends I'm okay with him having entertainment on the side? How do I trust him at all? More to the point—" she pressed her palms against her thighs and straightened "—why should I? And if you prefer being his secret emissary, why did you help me in the first place?"

"I'm not Trey's anything," he assured.

"All right then." She tightened the knot in her T-shirt with finality and tugged up the boots. "How far does the property go on the other side of the pond?"

"It doesn't."

"Is it private?" She raised her eyebrows. "Owned by the Fortune Trust, perhaps?"

His lips twitched. "Not owned by the Fortune Trust. But if you want to end up at Lake Chatelaine, keep going. It's only a few miles of barely passable rocky terrain. Considering your specialty footwear, there, it shouldn't take you long. You might make it by midnight."

"Just an easy little day hike. No thanks." She patted the head of the statue as she walked past it again. She passed the weathered bench, too. The wood had still been damp, easily working through the thin leggings. "I'm not having second thoughts about Trey. But I am thinking about that leftover piece of bacon back at the castle. It's been calling my name for at least an hour."

Isabel's hips swayed as she marched back into the sunlight. Maybe the sway was exaggerated because of having to maneuver in the oversize rubber boots.

Maybe not.

Either way, Reeve had no business focusing on it as much as he did. No matter what she said about Trey.

He patted the head of the statue the same way that Isabel had and easily caught up to her.

"How'd the two of you meet, anyway?" he asked.

"Maybe *you* should date Trey, you want to talk about him so much." She sighed noisily. "We met at a fundraiser two years ago. Our first date was a picnic on his family's yacht. He proposed nine months ago at a surprise birthday party he threw for me, complete with a mariachi band and sparklers."

"And you said yes."

"And I said yes. Isn't that what one does when the man you've been dating goes down on one knee in front of all his friends and family, offering up his heart?"

Or at least a spectacular ring. "But—?"

"Who says there's a but?"

"There's always a but when it comes to people like Trey. An excuse. A lie."

"So says the voice of experience. Who's lied to you?"

"I'm surrounded by people who lie. Who tell me what they think I want to hear."

"You're too cynical."

"I'm realistic. And experienced when it comes to people out to make an easy profit."

"Mariana Sanchez is not out to make an easy profit."

"I wasn't referring to Mariana Sanchez."

She gave him a disbelieving look. "Weren't you?"

"Not only her," he allowed.

Isabel was walking so quickly—evidently so anxious to get back to that last piece of bacon—that she didn't notice a fallen log when they came to it and would have pitched right over it if he hadn't caught her around the waist first.

She immediately pushed him away with a muttered "thank you," but not so immediately that he hadn't felt the warmth emanating from her skin.

He shoved his fingertips into his front pockets. He nearly pulled out the note of apology he'd retrieved from the study before he remembered what the crumpled paper was. He blamed Gigi for the sentimentality that had prompted him to write it in the first place.

He pushed it even deeper into his pocket. "I'd already been dealing with one claim against my grandfather when the Mariana situation came up."

"She's a person, not a situation."

Reeve wondered if Isabel listened to Gigi's podcast. She might have been quoting one of his sister's favorite phrases. "Do you want to hear my side or not?"

She looked oddly surprised. "Aren't you afraid I'll blog about it?" Her expression shifted. "Oh, wait. You've taken care of that problem by *buying* it."

He wondered why he'd expected anything different. He pulled his hands free again and stepped over the log. "Forget it."

She said something under her breath. "Wait. I'm sorry."

He looked over his shoulder at her, waiting while she stepped over the log with exaggerated care. Once across, she stomped her right boot as if she were settling her foot down into the boot again. "Yes, I do want to hear your side."

He didn't know where the urgency came from to explain his side of things. Generally, he didn't have to explain himself. The group of people who challenged him to do so was very small. But that urgency had been brewing since she'd admitted she was the brain behind *The Chatelaine Report.*

Was he trusting her too much? Or was he reeling out enough rope to see if she'd hang herself with it?

It disturbed him that he didn't know the answer to that. He wasn't used to uncertainty. It went against everything he'd ever learned from Walter—before his death and after.

But when it came to Isabel, there was very little that *was* certain. Except that Reeve wanted her. He had from the moment he'd met her...except she'd had eyes only for her new fiancé.

Her hair had dried in an untidy mass of glossy brown waves around her shoulders and her nose was slightly pink from the wash of sunshine. And there was nothing but curiosity shining now from those deep brown eyes.

Trust or rope?

He guessed he'd find out in time.

"Eighteen months ago," he began, "a woman from Italy came forward with what seemed to be legitimate proof that her grandmother had been involved with Walter during the war. Second World War, that is. Except she had a more novel approach than most. She wasn't claiming she was the progeny of their union. That's almost commonplace. Happened with my grandfather. Happened with my father. Always been able to disprove it. Blood tests. Witnesses."

"DNA," she inserted, obviously still thinking of her pet cause named Mariana Sanchez.

"DNA," he said, allowing her the point. "In a way, what Paola Agnoli claimed was worse—that Walter had gone AWOL and in exchange for her grandmother helping him stay hidden from his command, he'd written her a letter promising to sign the title of one of the Fortune mines over to her."

"AWOL! Your great-grandfather was a decorated war hero."

"How'd you know that?"

She made a face. "Despite what you think, I'm not all fluffy gossip. I do know how to research."

He contained the "not well enough" that automatically reared its head.

"Absent without leave should have been easy enough to disprove because of his service record," she went on. "So what was the catch?"

"There were a few days in 1943 when Walter and five other guys from his unit seemed to fall off the map."

Her lips parted.

"Yeah. I didn't even tell Gigi the details."

"She's your sister! Why not?"

"You tell your sisters everything?"

"Just about."

"You're women. It's different."

"Whatever." She rolled her eyes. "But still, she's Walter's great-grandchild, too. Seems like she has as much a personal stake as you do."

"Yeah, but she worshipped the old man."

"And you didn't?" She lifted her arms. "I've been around you less than twenty-four hours and I can tell otherwise."

"It would have broken her heart if Agnoli's claim turned out to be true. Not because of having to share the mine or the ancillary profits ever since, but because it would be proof of Walter's fallibility. The war hero turning out to be a fake?" He grimaced. "It would have hurt her unnecessarily."

She shaded her eyes with her hand as she looked up at him. "Was he a fake?"

"No, but at the time, I couldn't prove it conclusively. I'd already spent months keeping the case under the radar—both from Gigi *and* from being made public—and along comes Mariana Sanchez insisting on meeting me. And then, I come to find out that she'd been bugging my sister for months before that. I didn't have any tolerance left to deal with another attack on Walter's character." He gave her a pointed look. "I still don't."

Oblivious to his warning, Isabel stepped in his path. "I've talked to Mariana. I'm certain she's not out to attack anyone. I honestly believe she is not motivated by profit. She just wants to *meet* you!"

"Whatever she's out for, she can deal with our attorneys," he said flatly.

Isabel's lips compressed, but she dropped it. "What happened about your grandfather? Did he really write that letter?"

"The handwriting experts didn't conclusively state that he had. And they didn't conclusively state that he hadn't. Which is why the case lasted as long as it did. But the investigators I hired were finally able to get to the bottom of those missing days."

"*Had* he gone AWOL after all?"

"No. He was part of a small team that had been dispatched in secret to smuggle some information up the line. But it was totally off the books, which is why it looked as suspicious as it did."

"Then how did you corroborate his whereabouts? Or even know about the mission in the first place?"

"All throughout the war, he continued writing in

his journals. He served for four years. Four journals."
He had them all. Just not the one year before the war
that PJ wanted. "Walter never specifically mentioned
the Salerno mission, but he talked about the guys he
served with. The ones he trusted the most. The ones
he didn't. My investigators tracked down the survi-
vors of every person he'd mentioned, and with bits
from one person and bits from another, they eventually pieced together a path to the daughter of the contact who'd received that secret message."

"Impressive."

Reeve paid them well to be impressive. "The
daughter even remembered the day when a ragtag
handful of American soldiers came trudging through
their field. She was a little girl then, but not only was
she able to identify nearly all the men who'd met with
her father, she produced a photograph from her father's effects of the men celebrating. Walter was right
there in the middle of them, plain as day. He couldn't
have been signing and dating a letter for someone in
Salerno when, for days, he'd been making his way a
hundred miles away. On foot."

"No wonder you love the journals."

"They've proved handy a time or two," he agreed
mildly. "And after a year and a half of fighting to
preserve Walter's reputation, I finally won. Agnoli's
case was dismissed about six weeks ago."

"You must have been relieved."

"For Gigi's sake. It's resolved and she never needs
to know about it at all, or about how close we came
to it going the other way." He shrugged.

She tsked. "Why pretend you're only glad for your sister's sake? Your faith in Walter continues, unshaken."

"I don't know about faith. But I do know Walter. Duty and honor colored everything that mattered to him. Doesn't matter what the Sanchez woman believes. He wouldn't have had a child he never acknowledged."

"Not deliberately, from the sounds of it. But what if he didn't know? Even you must admit that a person can't know *everything*. A youthful indiscretion that results in a pair of baby booties? It's been happening since the dawn of time. She has DNA test results, Reeve. Two of them! They both confirm she's a cousin of Wendell's grandchildren."

"That doesn't mean she's *Walter's* grandchild," he said flatly. "I just told you there were other brothers."

"Who are nowhere to be found! But you and your sister are right here and if you were just willing to meet her—maybe shed some light on the situation?" She reached out and grabbed his wrist. "Maybe you'll be right. But even if you're not, it doesn't mean your great-grandfather wasn't still the man you admire."

Reeve looked down at her slender fingers squeezing his wrist. They were long. Warm. Feminine.

And as if she'd suddenly realized what she'd done, she let go and cupped her hand around her opposite shoulder. She turned and started for the castle again. "I wonder if that secret mission of your grandfather's was a pivotal moment in the war. That would be something, wouldn't it? It's too bad he didn't elaborate more in his journals."

Reeve followed her slowly. A ring of heat lingered around his wrist. It was distracting. "Like you said. There are a lot of years unaccounted for."

"Is that what you were looking for in that box? Another journal from the missing years?"

"It's what I always look for when I come to the castle." And it had nothing to do with PJ.

She gave him a quick glance over her shoulder. "Like a treasure hunt."

"Yeah." He smiled slightly. She had a sparkle in her eyes again. "You want to help look?"

Chapter Eight

What was wrong with him?

You want to help look?

Reeve couldn't even retract the thoughtless question because Isabel was already nodding eagerly. "I'd love to help!"

He shoved his fingers back in his pockets again.

"I mean, I might as well do something useful for you this afternoon," she added more diffidently.

"I wasn't suggesting you needed to hunt through closets and drawers to earn your keep."

"I know." They'd nearly reached the steps and she walked more quickly, giving her boots another tug. "It's a good way to stay distracted. though."

The reason she sought distraction was something Reeve needed to remember. Maybe tediously working through a closet or two would provide a well-needed distraction for him, too.

Along the way, he could tattoo on his brain that she was not available.

"Where have you found them up to now?"

"You name it. In the cellar under a case of old fuses. Sitting inside a cold fireplace in one of the bedrooms."

"Do you think he was sticking them in odd places because it amused him or was he, uh—"

"—starting to lose it?" He shook his head. "He was entirely sane to the day he died. If there was a message behind the locations where he hid his journals, it's too obscure for me to figure out."

"Any relationship between where you've found them and what was going on at the time he was writing in that particular journal?"

"Not that I noticed."

"You were just happy to lay your hands on another opportunity to take a trip with your gramps."

He couldn't help a short laugh. "He was never gramps to me. Grampy to Gigi. To me, he was 'Grandfather.'"

"So formal."

He shrugged. "He was grooming me to run the family business, not teaching me how to tie a fishing fly."

"Did he fish?"

"In one of the later journals—he was probably eighty—he wrote about fishing when he'd been young. He grew up with some heavy expectations from *his* father, too." Namely the fact that he married well. Very well. Effie Sutherland from New York had fit the bill. "I don't think he had a lot of time on his hands that hadn't already been planned out for him."

They'd reached the base of the stairs and she started up them.

Next time he bought her clothes, they were going to be as shapeless as a sack.

He let her get about a dozen steps ahead of him just so he wasn't at eye level with her perfect rear end as she quickly ascended the steps.

"What about you?" She sounded slightly breathless. "Any fishing in your past? What does Reeve Fortune, CEO of not one, but count 'em two, successful corporations do for enjoyment? Or is it all about the basketball court?"

"Basketball is so I don't get frozen in place sitting on my ass in endless meetings," he said drily. "If I want to really enjoy something, I go sailing."

She paused and looked back at him. "You sail?"

"I have homes on Lake Chatelaine and Aransas Pass. I can walk out to the water at both. Yeah, I sail. Boat. Surf. Water-ski." Admittedly, it'd been a while since he'd managed to do any of those things because Cora kept his calendar too damn busy.

Meanwhile, Isabel was staring at him like he'd grown a second nose.

"What?"

"I'm just…" She lifted a shoulder. "You surprised me."

"Why? Because I can get wet and not melt?"

"I guess the only other times I've seen you so... sporty...was when I've gone to see—" She broke off.

"Trey?"

She moistened her lips. "Y'all were always playing basketball at the gym."

"I know."

Something in her dark eyes flickered. "I always wanted to learn how to sail. But we got golf lessons and cotillion instead."

"Not so different from my youth."

"Except our golf lessons were from our dad."

"And cotillion?"

"Mom's on the committee." Her lips curved wryly. "We went to public school and didn't have family vacations on the Amalfi Coast."

"At least you had family vacations." The admission revealed more than he wanted. "I'll take the water over all of it. I can watch the sunrise over the water from my bed."

She produced a forced smile. "That's, uh, that's... good for you." She turned and darted up the rest of the steps, not even stopping when she had to pull up her boots along the way.

He took his time catching up to her.

Mostly so she wouldn't see the smile that he suddenly couldn't seem to control.

Despite her claim about the beckoning bacon, she bypassed the kitchen altogether and returned to the study.

"We need a plan," she said. "Do you have a floor plan of this place?"

He nearly laughed. "No."

"Okay, then we'll just have to draw one up." She started to open the desk drawer, but hesitated, giving him a quick look. "Do you mind?"

He was curious to see what she would do. He waved his hand. "Go for it."

She pulled the drawer open and sifted through the clutter until she finally pulled out a pad of yellowing paper. She riffled through it. "Only a few sheets left, but we'll make do." She poked a little more. "This stuff in here is really old."

"It's a really old desk."

She gathered her hair up with both hands and shut the drawer with her hip as she wove a mother-of-pearl letter opener through the ponytail, capturing it into a messy knot. Then she sat beside him on the sofa with the pad of paper and handed it to him along with the stubby pencil. "Have you been methodical when you've searched before?" She sucked in her lower lip, waiting expectantly.

"I'm a methodical man." He looked away from her mouth and thought of freezing showers. "What do you think?"

"Okay." She tapped the pad of paper. "Have you searched the top floor?"

"The third floor of the main house, but not the towers or turrets."

"Sorry, but towers and turrets sound like perfect hiding places to me."

He smiled slightly. "The tower staircases are all

narrow and winding. I'm not sure anyone has ever
been up to the turrets. Much less Walter."

"Don't you think we should at least rule them out?"
She didn't wait for an answer. "Just draw a map of
the castle."

He chuckled. "There's not enough paper here for
that." But he began sketching the main portion of the
castle with the great hall at its center. "Most of the
place will be easy to cross off. Hard to hide a journal
in an entirely empty room."

"But most of the rooms *aren't* empty," she argued.
She drew up one knee and turned toward him. "The
foyer alone was filled with stuff. That suit of armor
by the staircase? If I were going to hide something,
that'd be the first place I'd think of."

Which was likely the very reason that Walter Fortune wouldn't have, but Reeve didn't say so. And what
did it hurt to think outside his particular box? It would
be more likely that Walter would have dropped one of
his journals down inside a set of armor than hidden it
above, on the narrow interior balcony that protected
the base of the stained-glass windows.

Before long, he'd drawn what he could given the
limited supply of paper. She pulled on the rubber
boots again and they set out, stopping by the kitchen
only long enough for her to eat that piece of bacon.

Three hours later, Reeve had to acknowledge that
his method of looking for something was considerably different from Isabel's. Where he would walk

through a room, open a closet or a drawer, she would crawl right under a bed and come out with dust bunnies clinging to her not-so-bright pink shirt. She lifted mattresses. She made him not just open drawers but pull them all the way out to make sure nothing had fallen behind. She ran her hands down closet walls to find loose panels and lifted rugs to peek beneath.

It was impressive. But fruitless.

They'd crossed five rooms off the map before they approached the first tower.

The winding concrete steps were built into the outer wall and were so narrow, Reeve told Isabel to go ahead of him.

"Why have a tower at all," she said, her voice echoing down to him, "if the only thing in it are stairs like this?"

"You'd have had to ask Wendell that," he said. His right shoulder brushed against the wall, giving him a sense of claustrophobia despite the open center of the tower that was crisscrossed every so often with a beam. Mostly, he was thinking about having to go back down the treacherous stairs.

The descent was always harder than the ascent and there wasn't a railing at all. Given the fact that Wendell had built the castle in modern times, he could have at least had stairs with a central pole in his purposeless towers.

"I think this might be the turret," Isabel said eventually and was standing in front of an access panel when he stopped a few steps below her.

He leaned out from the curved wall and looked up.

The stairs wound upward for another good fifteen feet before they appeared to stop.

Destination nowhere.

He looked back at the panel in front of Isabel. "Can you move it? Try pushing on it. Or sliding it."

She tried both. The panel was smooth wood. No fingerholds or anything else to aid opening it. "It's not budging." She came down a step. "You should try."

He didn't believe for a minute that his grandfather would have tried to get up the tower, much less into the turret that projected from the side of it.

But Isabel was looking down at him with such expectation in her dark brown eyes, he swallowed his logic. "You'll have to get below me," he told her, and flattened himself as much as he could against the wall so she could get past him.

"This is, um, pretty tight," she muttered as she came down another step.

It was pretty damn stupid, too, but he'd been the one to open this particular can of worms. They couldn't both stand on the same step at the same time. He stretched out his arm against the wall and beckoned with his fingers. "Come on. You're going to have to step around me. I'll hold you."

"These boots aren't making things easier," she muttered, and she grabbed his arm with one hand while she tugged one of them off and sent it plummeting down the center of the tower, thudding occasionally against the crossbeams. It was followed by the other. "That's better," she said breathlessly.

Maybe for her.

Her hand followed his arm until it reached his shoulder and then her stocking-clad foot slid over his boots and her thigh brushed against his as she sought the next step. Her head passed beneath his chin, and he wrapped his arm around her back to keep her steady.

There was no way to avoid pressing against each other in the process, so he didn't bother trying. Neither did she. But finally, her feet were safely on the step below his and her forehead pressed against his other arm for a moment. Her fingers still dug into his shoulder.

"Why did I think this was a good idea?"

A half laugh escaped him. He wasn't going to forget the lithe warmth of her or that racing heartbeat of hers anytime soon. "Hell if I know." He inhaled deeply and blew it out. "You good?"

"Yeah." Her grip loosened slightly, and she lifted her head. "I'm, um, I'm good." She went down another step before letting go of him altogether, and through sheer effort, he turned his attention away from her and to the panel.

He pushed on it the same way that she had. He tried sliding it with the palms of his hands the same way that she had. It didn't move for him any more than it had for her.

He ran his fingertips around the edges and finally, at the very bottom of it, he felt a depression. "Give me that letter opener in your hair." He held out his hand.

She immediately pulled it out and placed it on his

palm like a surgical tool. He inserted the sharp tip into the depression and pushed.

With a soft *snick*, the door swung inward an inch. He returned the letter opener to her and pushed open the panel the rest of the way. He had to angle his shoulders to fit through the narrow opening and once he was inside the turret, he couldn't straighten all the way without hitting his head on the ceiling that was much lower than the conical exterior would have suggested.

Isabel, however, was able to slip right through and she quickly joined him inside the round room.

The turret had a diameter of maybe twelve feet, with narrow slitted windows on the walls. In another era, they would have had an actual defensive purpose. Now, they were as uselessly aesthetic as the entire tower.

A wood bench with an inlaid pattern of gold leaves ran the circumference of the room and Isabel knelt on it as she looked out one of the windows. "Talk about a place for dreaming." She sounded wistful.

Dreams didn't get far. Action did. "There's no way a journal is hidden in here, Isabel."

She looked over her shoulder at him. She'd wrapped her hair back up with the letter opener and the mother-of-pearl handle glinted pink and blue in the light through the window. "I realize that. But still, it's quite something, isn't it?" She spread her arms and giggled. "I mean, we're standing in a castle turret!"

"We're standing in a turret of a castle that's not really a castle."

She left the bench. "How is this *not* a real castle?"

"No royalty. No purpose for defending land or title. I don't know. *Wendell* was the one who was fascinated with them."

She propped her hands on her hips. "I think you have a serious lack of imagination."

He snorted softly. "Sweetheart, I can imagine plenty."

Her eyes widened slightly, and color bloomed on her cheeks.

Then he made the mistake of straightening and cracked his head right through the surface of the ceiling.

"Reeve!" Isabel hurried over to him, brushing at the debris that rained down on his shoulders. "Are you all right?"

"It didn't hurt." He cautiously hunched his head down again, keeping his eyes shut tight. "It's just a lot of dust." His eyes were already watering.

"Sit." Her hands grabbed his shoulders as she directed him to the bench. "Should I try wiping your face? Are you wearing contact lenses?"

"I don't wear contacts. Wait a sec." He bent forward and pulled his T-shirt over his head, turning it inside out as he did so. Then he was able to use the clean side to wipe his face.

He still felt grit inside his eyes when he opened them.

"Let them water." She stilled his hands before he could rub them, but just as quickly released him and moved across the room toward the access panel.

It was obvious she wanted to keep as much distance between them as the turret allowed.

"Relax. I didn't mean anything by the *sweetheart*. It's a bad habit of mine," he lied. "My sister's always trying to school me on it. 'People have names. Use them.'"

"Sweetheart's a lot better than princess," she muttered. "And my dad has always called my mom darling, so I guess there's an argument either way. Of course, they've been married forever. You know what? Forget it."

"What's a 'sweetheart' here and there between friends?" He couldn't help but smile. He squeezed his eyes shut and opened them again, blinking away the watering as much as he could.

They still burned, but at least he could see enough to get back down the tower stairs.

He shook out his shirt and turned it right side out once more. Then he squinted up at the hole he'd left in the ceiling. He could clearly see through it to the interior beams that formed the cone-shaped roof.

If it weren't for the miserable method of reaching it, the turret—sans ceiling—*would* make for an intriguing space.

A private office. One that would discourage constant interruptions.

A cozy bedroom for the same reasons. No interruptions.

His mind immediately went down that particular rabbit hole. Hard for it not to when Isabel was only a couple yards away.

Mentally he slammed down a metal plank before he could dig any deeper down that hole than he already had.

He yanked his shirt over his shoulders and stood again, holding his head even lower than before. "Let me go first," he told Isabel.

"Are you sure?" She didn't move. "Can you see well enough? Maybe we should wait."

"I can see. And yes, I'm sure. Going down will be worse than coming up. If you lose your footing, I'll be able to catch you."

"I'm not going to lose my— Wait. *That's* why you wanted me to go first when we came up here?"

"Things fall *down*, Isabel. It's called gravity." She still hadn't budged, and he reached for her shoulders, ready to move her aside.

She moved quickly then. No doubt to evade his touch.

Just as well. He'd never been a masochist. Touching her wasn't going to lead anywhere useful and that pseudo-sexual dance on the stairs getting up here had nearly done him in.

He angled through the narrow opening again and went down several steps before stopping to be sure she was safely following.

When she stepped out of the turret, her feet were bare of the socks he'd given her.

"Naked is better," she mumbled.

He nearly choked, even though he knew she only meant that her bare feet would have a better grip on the stairs.

"Should I try to pull the panel closed again?"

The last thing he cared about was that panel. "Leave it. I'm going to have to get someone out to fix the ceiling anyway." He might control the Fortune Trust, but he didn't have the right to leave any portion of the castle damaged. Not even in a location that would probably never be visited by anyone except the two of them.

His eyes were still watering but not so badly that he couldn't see where he was going, and he started down the stairs.

They were nearly halfway down the tower stairs when he felt Isabel on the step directly behind him. She grabbed the back of his shirt and he stopped.

"Did you hear that?" Her voice whispered close to his ear.

"What?"

She scooted even closer to him. "Someone's down there."

He shook his head. "You're imagining things." Whereas he wasn't imagining the press of her soft breasts against his shoulder blades at all.

He went down another step, but so did she. Sticking to him like a limpet.

He was going to be an old man by the time they made it back down all the stairs.

"Relax," he told her. "There's nobody here but—" He broke off, just as he felt her hand twist his shirt even tighter. Her knuckles burned sweetly against his spine but even that wasn't distraction enough to miss the noise that he *did* hear coming from somewhere below.

"I told you," she whispered urgently. Her lips brushed his ear.

He didn't know if he hated the tower stairs or loved them. "It's probably just Smitty." He leaned away from the wall enough to look down but all he could see was the next coil of spiraling stairs. He reached behind him to transfer her death grip from his shirt to his hand. "The caretaker I mentioned."

Her fingers wound around his. She followed up with her other hand, too. She really was alarmed. "The one you said usually checks on things at *night*?"

"Don't worry so much," he assured. "People don't trespass out here."

"*You* climbed in through a window," she said under her breath. "Think you're the only one to figure that one out?"

She had a point.

Standing there on the stairs doing nothing went against the grain too much, though, and Reeve started moving again. His own footfalls struck him as loud on the steps, but the feel of Isabel huddling close behind him was the loudest distraction.

He had to remind himself more than once that it was also a pointless distraction. She was motivated by an overactive imagination. Not by an overwhelming desire for someone besides her fiancé.

They circled the tower twice more before Reeve could see light at the center far below. "Almost there."

"And then what?"

He didn't answer. Telling her how badly he needed a cold shower wasn't going to do either of them any good.

"Who goes there?" A gravelly voice shouted up at them, followed by the clanging of metal on metal. "I'm warning you. I've got a crowbar here and I know how t'use it."

Relaxing, Reeve let go of Isabel's hand. Only to tense up again when she slipped several fingers through one of his belt loops.

He cleared a sudden frog from his throat. "Smitty?" He leaned over, trying to see the man below, and nearly groaned out loud at the way Isabel leaned with him. "It's Reeve. Reeve Fortune."

"Reeve?" The voice scoffed. "Reeve doesn't come out here."

"Sure I do." He couldn't see the man and he straightened. Isabel straightened along with him.

And he'd thought going *up* the stairs had been an exercise in torture.

He went down another group of stairs. "I was here a couple winters ago," he called gruffly. "I left a box of cigars in the office for you."

A grunt of acknowledgment made its way to them. "You bring another box?"

He smiled and felt Isabel finally relax.

She let go of his belt loop. He could only hope his ability to breathe normally returned sometime this century.

"Not yet," he managed to call out as they continued their descent.

"Well, don't bother," Smitty returned. "Can't smoke those things anymore."

Reeve hid his shock when the old man came into view.

Smitty hadn't been lying about the crowbar. But he looked as if he'd aged a decade in the last few years. Once tall and hearty, he was now skinny and stooped. His grizzled beard couldn't hide his sunken cheeks, and what hair was left on his head had gone thin and gray.

His gaze was nevertheless still sharp when it landed on Isabel coming down behind Reeve.

He gave Reeve a speculative look. "Whatcha been doing up there in the tower?"

"Satisfying my curiosity," Isabel said, slipping around Reeve to skip down the last few steps. She reached out her hand to the caretaker. "Isabel Banninger. It's nice to meet you, Mr. Smitty."

The old man shook the tips of her fingers as if he was afraid of causing her damage. "Just Smitty, Ms. Banninger."

"Isabel's staying here a few days," Reeve told him.

Smitty's eyebrows climbed into his wrinkled forehead. "Is she now?" He released her fingertips and leaned on the long black crowbar as if it were a cane. "Hope you're using the Silver Suite."

"She slept in the old study," Reeve said.

"What the hell for? Beg pardon, miss," he added quickly.

Isabel just looked bemused.

Smitty propped the crowbar against the wall and

yanked a handkerchief from his back pocket. He
swiped his forehead with it. "The Silver Suite is the
finest room we got here," he told Isabel. "I always
keep it polished up just in case."

"In case of *what*?"

"The name alone sounds lovely." Isabel sent Reeve
a look from slightly disapproving eyes.

Smitty's head bobbed. "I'd be happy to show you.
Some mighty fine people have slept in that room."

Maybe sixty years ago, Reeve thought silently.

"I'd love to hear more," Isabel told him.

Smitty looked about ready to preen. "The first
lady herself spent an evening here in Mr. Wendell's
company."

"Really!" Isabel tucked her hand through the arm
that the old guy offered. "The first lady of Texas?"

"None other, miss. There's a photograph in the
office."

"Reeve mentioned the office."

"Office. Library. Dozens of rooms and all of them
more suitable for guests than that tiny study." Smitty
gave Reeve a pointed look.

"It had what she needed," he defended.

"I've been fine," Isabel assured quickly. "I needed
a place to get away and that's exactly what I got."

"Well." Smitty sniffed and patted her hand. "Come
with me and I'll tell you all about the castle." His
faded blue gaze took in Reeve as well. "Built at the
height of the silver mining days, it's a marvel. But the
one thing it's never truly had was a woman's touch."

Chapter Nine

"You're sure you're okay with this?"

Isabel looked at Reeve. It was Monday morning, and they were parked at the curb outside her apartment building in Chatelaine. "I can't hide out at Wendell's Folly forever."

Trey—miserable, lying, cheating Trey—had always called her his princess.

How strange it was that she'd actually *felt* like one the night before, sleeping in the luxurious Silver Suite at the castle.

"Well, you *could*," Reeve countered, looking wry. "But Smitty might talk your ear off. Guy's never been that chatty with me."

"I *did* ask him to tell me all about the castle."

"And he did," Reeve said. "For hours."

She couldn't help a soft laugh. "True enough." The

man had seemed prepared to talk endlessly about the construction of the castle and the various elements that had been incorporated by Wendell Fortune's builders. He'd only stopped when she'd finally claimed exhaustion. It hadn't been entirely an exaggeration on her part. "I'm sorry we didn't find any more of Walter's journals, though."

He shrugged. "It was a long shot in the first place."

She held her breath slightly, wondering if he'd suggest they try again another time, but he didn't.

And she had no business feeling disappointed. It hadn't even been forty-eight hours since she'd been ready to marry another man.

Her judgment had clearly gotten out of whack, if she was imagining an attraction to Reeve Fortune.

It was probably just as well that he hadn't slept at the castle the night before. In fact, he'd hastily exited once they'd shared the grilled cheese sandwiches and tomato soup that Smitty had insisted on preparing for them.

She still wasn't sure if Reeve's departure had more to do with Smitty's nonstop chatter or with her, but Reeve had nevertheless been sitting in the small kitchen that morning, when she'd finally dragged herself from the sinful comfort of the Silver Suite and found her way through the maze of hallways.

Just like the day before, he'd brought breakfast. And he'd been reading the newspaper. Only the casual shirt and jeans were gone, replaced by suit and tie.

Unlike the tie he'd never put on for her wedding-that-wasn't, this one was tied precisely around his neck. His hair was slicked back from his forehead.

He looked every inch the CEO who'd bought out her blog and every other thing that had been controlled by Stellar Productions.

"Well." She rubbed her hands down the leggings. She'd rinsed them, along with the T-shirt, the night before under a waterspout shaped like a dolphin in a sink shaped like a seashell and left them on the balcony of her suite to dry. Both items were still slightly damp. "I, um—" She owed him for the rescue. She owed him for the respite even more. But suddenly, expressing it felt nearly impossible. "I'll send you a check for everything I owe you."

The corners of his mouth lifted fractionally. "You're welcome, Isabel."

She felt flushed and nodded jerkily. Her granny's delicate hanky, still wrapped around the hairpins, was tucked in the console and she lifted it out as she reached for the door handle.

"Put something in your blog," he suggested abruptly. "Get ahead of Trey on it while you can."

The last personal thing she'd written in *The Chatelaine Report* had been that it would be on hiatus for a couple of weeks while she went on her honeymoon. "My blog can't compete against the public relations team that his family's probably already put on it."

He shrugged. "You never know."

"Maybe I want to write about the fact that the guy threatening to sue me turned out to be my rescuer."

"I suppose you could. It's your blog."

Oh, the difference a few days could make.

"As long as I don't mention Mariana Sanchez," she added.

His lips twisted and she raised her hand quickly. "Don't worry. I'm not going to poke that bear again. Even though I think you're entirely wrong about her." She pushed open the car door and the warmth of the morning rushed into the air-conditioned interior. She looked back at him, then impetuously leaned over the console and pressed a quick kiss against his cheek.

He jerked as if she'd burned him with a hot poker. "What did you do that for?"

Her hand tightened around her hanky and pins. "Because you were unexpectedly decent," she managed lightly. "But don't worry. I won't let your secret out." Then, because she felt like an absolute idiot and her lips were still tingling from that brief contact, she climbed out of the car and quickly shut the door.

She didn't look back as she hurried up the short sidewalk to the apartment building, her high-heeled sandals clicking against the concrete.

She found her spare key in the potted geraniums below her windowsill, opened her door and went inside.

Only then did she hear his car drive away.

She leaned back against the door and blindly flipped the lock. "Isabel, you are *such* a mess."

The stack of packing boxes sitting forlornly against the far wall seemed to agree.

"And then what happened?" Ronnie's expression was avid as she helped spread the sheet on the bed that she and her husband had already returned to Isabel's apartment. "After you arrived at the castle?"

"Nothing happened." Isabel had pillowcases but no bed pillows to fill them since she'd donated them to a shelter, along with all the other housewares that she'd thought she wouldn't be needing post-marriage. "Reeve showed me around, we ate some pizza and he left." She purposely omitted the details that followed. She didn't want to talk about any of it until she'd had a chance to decide what she thought about it all.

But her chance of thinking had been truncated when Ronnie showed up at Isabel's door barely an hour after Reeve had driven away.

"Your landlady called me," Ronnie had said, pushing a tall cup of coffee into one of Isabel's hands and her overnight bag from the church into her other. She'd sidled past Isabel into the apartment, closely followed by their mom.

Isabel should have expected as much.

Now, Lydia Banninger was perched on a metal folding chair that they'd borrowed from Geraldine. Isabel figured that if Paige hadn't had to work, she'd have been there, too.

"I don't understand," her mother said. "Isn't this Reeve Fortune the one who wants to sue you?"

"It was just a threat, Mom."

"And he was a friend of Trey's?"

"They know each other."

"*And* you didn't particularly care for him?"

Isabel bent over and needlessly straightened the hospital corners of her sheets. "I didn't."

"Issa," Lydia said with a sigh. "What—"

"I don't know, Mom." She straightened. "Okay? I don't know anything except that marrying Trey would have been the biggest mistake of my life. Would you rather I'd have gone through with it?"

Her mother looked indignant. "Of course not. Frankly, I spent all weekend talking your daddy off a cliff. He wanted to go and beat the pants off Trey. It was difficult not letting on that I agreed with him."

"That would've been a sight." Ronnie sat on the corner of the bed. "I forgot to bring blankets."

"I need to go to GreatStore to buy a few pillows anyway," Isabel said. Then she needed furniture and other household items...

"Oh, Issa," Lydia chided softly. "The quality there is—"

"It's fine, Mom. Just because it's not from your favorite department store in Corpus doesn't mean their stuff's not good enough. And anyway, now that I'm not going to be Mrs. TFIII, shopping at GreatStore is going to be a lot friendlier to my budget." She sat down beside Ronnie. "Why did I let myself believe that Trey was something he's not?"

"You loved him," Ronnie said.

"Did I?" She threw herself back on the bed and stared up at the crack in the ceiling. "Or did I just love the idea of him?"

"Stop worrying about it," Lydia said. "It's done and over with and I'm not going to say I'm sorry. You're a lovely girl, Issa. One day, a man will come along who deserves you. Meanwhile, just put it right out of your mind."

That was Lydia Banninger's method. If she didn't like it, she didn't think about it.

"Now, let's go have lunch at that place that serves sides of steak," Lydia said firmly. "What's it called?"

"Saddle & Spur Roadhouse," Isabel provided, sitting up once more. It was a casual, homey place with reliably good food. Trey had never stepped foot in it. Or any other eatery around Chatelaine, for that matter.

"That's right." Her mom was studying her spread fingers. "Maybe afterward, we should have manicures. Your father's treat."

Isabel couldn't help but laugh. "Mom. We all just had mani-pedis for the wedding." She waggled her fingernails, which were still painted in ballet pink. The large diamond on her finger glinted in the light.

She slowly pulled the ring off her finger and held it up.

Prisms danced around the room.

"One more thing I'm going to have to return," she said with a sigh.

"I think you should keep it," Ronnie said. "It's the least he owes you."

Isabel smiled slightly. She appreciated Ronnie's stalwart support, even if she didn't happen to agree.

She pushed off the bed and went into the bathroom, where she stuck the ring inside her medicine cabinet for safekeeping. Then she went back into the bedroom. "I love you for being here, but can I get a rain check on lunch?" She gestured at the bed. "Blanket or no, all I can think of is grabbing some sleep." It was an excuse because if she told her mom she just wanted to be left alone, it would hurt her feelings.

"I'm sure you didn't sleep well at that drafty castle." Ronnie handed their mother her designer purse. "Admit it, Mom. You'd *love* to see the interior of a castle. It probably has your creative juices running over."

"Well, maybe I'm a *bit* curious."

Isabel tossed up her hands at the expectant look her mother gave her. "There's no earthly reason for me to go back there! And I'm certainly not going to ask Reeve about it. How would that look? I was practically married!"

Ronnie's eyebrows had climbed midway up her forehead. "Overreact much, Issa?"

"Don't listen to Ronnie." Lydia kissed Isabel's cheek. "She has no idea what it's like to have second thoughts."

Isabel and Ronnie both eyed their mother. "And *you* do?" Ronnie demanded.

"Not about your father," Lydia said, patting the wavy blond hair that she had passed on to all of her daughters except Isabel. "But I didn't spring from a seed with the express purpose of marrying your daddy. We had lives before *you,* you know."

"So sayeth the beauty queen," Ronnie said from the corner of her mouth. She nudged their mother toward the apartment door and looked back at Isabel. "Call if you want company when you go shopping."

She smiled faintly. "Pretty sure I can still manage the multitudinous aisles of GreatStore on my own. I'm not going to fall apart just because I'm not going to be Mrs. Trey Fitzgerald after all." She spread her hands. "Maybe I'll follow in Auntie Pearl's footsteps and *never* marry."

"Please don't aspire to be like my sister-in-law," Lydia said. She kissed Isabel's cheek again and tucked her arm through Ronnie's. "Just the idea of it makes me need wine. Do they serve it at Reins & Boots?"

"Boots & Saddle, Mom," Ronnie said.

"Saddle & Spur," Isabel corrected them both as she closed the door after them. She picked up the cup of coffee that she hadn't finished yet. She appreciated Ronnie's gesture. It was just Isabel's bad luck that it was a poor comparison to Reeve's coffee at Wendell's Folly.

She poured it down the kitchen drain and restlessly approached the stack of packing boxes in her living room. But opening them just reminded her of Reeve's box of old photographs and books.

She slapped the flaps closed again and picked up the overnighter that Ronnie had returned to her. She carried it into the bedroom and turned it upside down, dumping the contents out onto the bed. Then she pulled up the folding chair and sat down in front of it all.

She plucked her cell phone from the midst.

The battery was nearly dead.

But it had enough juice to tell her she had thirty-two missed phone calls and even more unread text messages. Half of them were from Trey.

She pressed the edge of the phone against her forehead. "Do *not* start feeling guilty now, Isabel."

But she was.

"Stupid," she muttered. For some masochistic reason, she'd saved a picture of the social media post, and it came right up when she opened her photo gallery.

Two days ago, she'd nearly thrown up at the sight of Trey kissing that naked girl.

Now she found herself wondering why the girl had subjected herself to the bachelor party in the first place. Had she needed the money? Had she been desperate for attention?

She pinched her eyes closed for a long minute.

At least seeing the photograph did the trick, magically dissolving any lurking kernels of regret.

She went back to her text messages, bypassing Trey's altogether.

Have you lost your mind?

Trey's telling everyone that you're sick. Is it true?

They spanned the gamut from accusatory to disbelief to concern.

Even as she held the phone, it pinged with another text message.

Princess, stop ignoring me. How many times do I have to tell you that it didn't mean any—

As if by divine timing, the screen went blank.

Battery dead.

She tossed the phone onto the bed and reached for the ridiculously brief length of beribboned lace that masqueraded as a negligee. She balled it up and threw it into the corner. "That doesn't mean anything either."

Then she carried her toiletries, neatly contained in a pretty little organizer, back to her bathroom and set everything in the medicine cabinet next to the diamond ring.

Could she get away with returning the ring by mail?

Messenger?

Carrier pigeon?

She closed the cabinet with a snap and went back to survey the rest of her stuff on the bed. Her honeymoon outfits were packed in a suitcase at Trey's. But the dress that she'd planned to wear for their morning-after breakfast was right there. She shook it out. No wrinkles, which was exactly the reason why she'd chosen it.

She exchanged the T-shirt and leggings for the coral-colored knit and pushed her feet into the pristine white tennis shoes.

Then she pulled her well-worn messenger bag from its hook in the closet, tucked her wallet and her dead phone inside next to the laptop that was already there, and swung the strap over her head as she left her apartment again.

Reeve had told her to get ahead of the story. And it was suddenly feeling like a very good thing to do.

As she walked to the Stellar Productions building, she couldn't help but look at the businesses along the way with a fresh eye, knowing that the land was all owned by the Fortune Trust.

Did Reeve know that Mrs. Sprague, who ran the Weed & Feed, had a daughter living in France who sent her croissants once a month? Or that Leo Hernandez was the third generation in his family to keep the shoe repair shop in business?

She waved through both storefronts as she passed them by. Across the street was the town museum that looked more like a white adobe house with a red-tiled roof than a museum and Connie Rios, the docent, was out front with a hose, watering the flowers growing in the planters. Isabel impetuously jaywalked across the quiet street. Connie had been one of the first people that Isabel had met when she'd moved to Chatelaine. Whenever Isabel wanted some historical bits about the town, she always started with Connie.

"Isabel!" Connie accidentally splashed water over herself. She quickly turned off the spigot. "Shouldn't you be on your honeymoon?"

Evidently, museum docents—even ones as young as Connie—were more interested in the past than in the current local gossip. "Let's just say there was a hitch on the way to the wedding. Your flowers look great."

Connie was obviously curious, but she was too polite to say anything. "Thank you. It's a wonder anything stays alive with this heat we're having." She tilted her head toward the shadowed doorway. "It's cool inside. Want to join me for some lemonade?"

Isabel wasn't particularly bothered by the heat, but she nodded. She hadn't started out with the museum in mind, but maybe it had been in her subconscious all along. "Sounds good."

There was no one inside the museum—not all that surprising. She followed Connie back to her office, stopping to look at the oversize map that hung on the hallway wall. Connie had told her once that it was more than a hundred years old. The street names were written in a faded spidery hand. The lines of the streets themselves were even more faded. "I hear there's an exhibit here about Fortune Metals."

"Sure." Connie gestured. "It's in the back room there. Only it's more about the Fortune Mining Company. Before it became the huge company it is now. You still blogging about the Fortunes? Your last one said you'd been threatened with legal action."

"Nice to know you keep up with reading it."

"Always." Connie came back out of her office carrying a pitcher of lemonade. "So, what happened?"

Isabel didn't want to get into the details. "It was dropped."

"Well, good. Just didn't sound like the Fortunes I know. They've always been generous where the museum is concerned. So, what do you want to know about the mining company?" She tapped a neat rectangle marked on the map. "Before it was moved out to the lake, the original mining office was right there."

The location seemed pretty far out of town, to Isabel. Or at least the town as it used to be. Some people claimed that Chatelaine never changed and maybe if you'd spent your entire life there, it would feel that way.

But the town that Isabel knew and the one lined out on the map were quite different. "What about the actual mine?"

Connie tapped a spot farther up toward the corner of the map. "All those red circles mark various mines that were in the area. In the late fifties and early sixties, competition was particularly fierce between Fortune Mining and Joyride Mining. Hold on." She went back into her office for a moment and returned without the pitcher but holding a glossy brochure. "This has a more complete map of all the abandoned mines in the area if you're into day hikes and such."

Isabel was less interested in a glossy map than she was the history of it all, but she took the brochure anyway. "Thanks." She slipped it into the pocket of her messenger bag. "You must know about the Fortune castle, too."

"I know a little. Toured it once when I was in elementary school." Connie smiled ruefully. "Would make a heck of a museum in comparison to this old place."

"Know anything about the man who built it?"

"Wendell Fortune? He was the youngest son of Jensen Fortune, who founded the mining company." She went back into her office but continued talking. "Richer than Midas, of course. All of them were." She returned with the lemonade, poured it into two plastic glasses filled with ice and handed one to Isabel.

"Thanks."

"Strange to think how much wealth poured out of the mines around here," Connie mused. She tipped her head back as she looked up at the circles near the corner of the map. "Not to mention death." She caught Isabel's questioning glance. "Mining accidents. They've always been a real thing. The Fortune mine was no exception. It collapsed once. Killed a lot of people." She shrugged fatalistically. "But people had to work. There was still a deep deposit of silver to be mined. If the Fortunes didn't do it, the Joyride would have."

"Fortune Metals is obviously still thriving. What about the Joyride?"

"Nothing left but an abandoned mine and a tour," Connie said. "If Wendell hadn't been rolling in profits, I doubt he could have built a castle purely for the whimsy of it." Then her smile turned mischievous. "Can't hold too much judgment over the Fortunes, though. Like I said. They're good to the museum. The Fortune Trust donates *quite* a tidy sum every year to help keep this place in operation."

The bell over the door tinkled softly and Connie quickly set her drink back inside her office before going out to greet the newcomers.

Isabel finished her own drink before moving into the back room. The "exhibit" comprised a series of enlarged photographs on the wall chronicling the rise—and some would say fall—of silver mining in the region. Even without Connie's commentary, it would have been obvious that Fortune Mining had survived and flourished when all other comers went by the wayside.

She studied a photograph of a young Walter Fortune. The similarity to Reeve was evident. Both in coloring and bearing. She moved on to another photo of Walter, now middle aged and standing alongside two young men. His son, Philip, and his brother, Wendell, according to the caption. And all blessed with good Fortune genes, she thought to herself.

There were pictures of mine workers sitting in the shade, clearly on a break with their big lunch boxes, and even more pictures of equipment. She peered through the glass of a case displaying chunks of rock containing veins of silver—at least according to the small description on the card next to them. Yellowed newspaper clippings pronounced Jobs Available! as well as Tragedy Strikes Fortunes Again below a photograph of Effie Fortune's funeral.

There were commentaries on the competitiveness between the Fortune Mining Company and Joyride Mining, and their involvement in a particularly colorful gubernatorial race.

Which only reminded her of Trey. His father had an eye on state politics.

There were even more newspaper clippings, but Isabel had seen enough.

Connie was still busy chatting with the two elderly women who'd come in and Isabel quietly left with a wave.

She crossed the street again and went around the corner to the Stellar Productions building. Seanmarie wasn't at her desk near the front door, and nobody paid Isabel any attention as she went down the hall. A red light outside of the recording studio warned that it was in use. She glanced in the doorway of the office belonging to Diana Dawson and was relieved to see that her personal stuff was still on the shelves.

Since FortuneMedia's acquisition, Isabel had been only one of many who'd feared that Diana would take her money and run. Maybe it was still in her plans, but for now, her framed college degree was still hanging on the wall in its usual spot.

Isabel continued to the rear of the converted house where a communal workspace was set up, equipped with copiers and phones and a variety of computers. She didn't need to use a computer, but she did need the internet since she'd already had it disconnected at her apartment.

She booted up her laptop, plugged in her phone to charge, and stuck a pod in the coffee maker. Lemonade was fine, but caffeine was her drink of choice.

By the time it was done brewing, her computer was up and running and her phone had enough life to produce a tiny blue light in the corner.

She sat down in front of the laptop and opened a new document.

But despite her intended topic she could only stare at the blank page.

Who is that bride running down the street? Why, it's Isabel Banninger, that's who. No ring. No vows. But the bliss? There's plenty of that, knowing I won't be marrying a lying, cheating—

Delete. Delete Delete. She hit the key again and again until only the cursor on the screen was blinking at her.

After nearly an hour of starting and deleting, she gave up and closed the laptop. She just wasn't ready to write about her wedding-that-wasn't.

She reached for her bag and wrote out a check to pay Reeve for the clothes and the food and sealed it inside an envelope from the box of them stored tidily on a shelf next to Stellar Productions letterhead. She wrote Reeve's name on the front and went back down the hall to Diana's office.

This time, the woman herself was behind her desk.

"Isabel!" Diana looked stunned. "What're you doing here? I thought you'd still be in the hospital. How are you feeling?"

"Fine, since I haven't been *in* the hospital." Isabel held up the envelope. "This is for Reeve Fortune. Do you expect to be seeing him at some point?"

"We had a delivery of some office furniture last Friday, so I figure he'll be showing up sooner or later."

She took an involuntary step through the doorway. "Surely he's not kicking you out of your office!"

Diana shook her head. "Actually, he's asked for me to stay on."

Diana was the best kind of success story—a woman who had succeeded through determination, skill and hard work. Now, instead of feeling defensive on her behalf, Isabel was forced to recalibrate some of her thinking. "You can do that? Sell your business to him and stick around to watch someone else be in charge?"

The other woman shook her head. "But that's just it. I will remain in charge." Her lips twitched slightly. "Only now I have a *monstrously* healthy bank balance and I'll also collect a paycheck from FortuneMedia." She shrugged her shoulders. "I've weighed the arguments and have decided I'd be a fool not to at least give it a chance. Now…" She folded her hands atop her desk and leaned forward. "Tell me what really happened between you and Mr. Wonderful."

"Don't pretend you haven't heard."

Diana spread her fingers slightly. "I've heard lots of gossip from lots of quarters. At the moment, the story with the most speed is that you had an emotional breakdown, which I can see for myself is baloney."

"But explains the supposed hospitalization." Isabel plopped down into one of the chairs in front of Diana's desk. "I changed my mind about getting married. Can we just leave it at that?"

Diana was clearly still curious, but she hid it well. "I'll show my selfish side and admit that I'm glad I won't be losing another voice behind *The Chatelaine Report.* You were like a godsend after Marguerita retired."

"I told you I hadn't planned to quit."

"As far as I can tell, people like Trey Fitzgerald tend to have little attention for some things. I'm sure he'd expect his wife to focus her energy on bigger and better things than a community blog. You would have left eventually." Diana's eyes searched hers. "If he were the man who truly deserved you, I'd have been happy for your marriage. Now… I'm happy for me. But *are* you okay?"

Isabel looked over her shoulder. There was nobody in the hallway behind them. She moistened her lips and looked back at Diana. "I feel *so* okay that I feel guilty about feeling so okay," she admitted in a whisper.

Diana's smile widened. "In my opinion, that's nothing that a good massage wouldn't cure."

Reeve had great hands. He'd probably—

She cut off *that* train of thought a little too late but still managed a wry smile. "You and my mother would agree on that."

"Sorry to interrupt." Looking rushed and worried, Seanmarie poked her head into the office. "The sign is here."

Diana's smile suddenly seemed a little forced as she stood. "I guess I should go see it then."

Isabel and Seanmarie followed in her wake. "I heard you were in a car accident," Seanmarie whispered to her. "But you look just fine."

"No accident. Not sick. Just decided not to get married."

"*Why?* Men like Trey Fitzgerald—"

"Can we not talk about it right now, Seanmarie?"

Seanmarie pouted slightly. They filed through the front door and out to the sidewalk in front of the house where three guys on ladders were affixing the long, narrow FortuneMedia sign.

Seanmarie was the first to speak. "Looks huge." She wrinkled her nose.

"It's no bigger than the Stellar Productions sign was," Diana countered.

"Plus it looks too modern," Seanmarie added.

Isabel had to agree. The silver letters were clean and spare on the black background and looked completely at odds with the lines of the quaint old house.

If she hadn't spent the last two days basically under Reeve Fortune's protection, she would have thought that it looked exactly the way she'd expect it to look from someone who gobbled up small companies left and right. Cold and emotionless.

"Modern or not, we'd all better get used to it." Diana marched back toward the front door. "Seanmarie, break out the cookies early today. I'm feeling the need for something that feels normal."

"I had the delivery guys put Reeve's office furniture in Stu's space," Diana told Isabel as they headed back through the house.

She startled. "Where did Stu go?" He'd been the crossword puzzle author for years.

"He quit last Friday. Said he'd worked for one big corporation and wasn't interested in working for another."

"Will you replace him?"

Diana shook her head. "FortuneMedia already has syndicated puzzles that we can use in any of our publications, digital and print."

"I *hate* all these changes," Seanmarie muttered as she stomped into the breakroom. Isabel could hear her slamming things around.

"Change," Diana murmured. "It's never easy."

She patted Isabel's shoulder and went into her office, pushing the door closed behind her.

Isabel flipped the envelope between her fingers and finally went upstairs to Stu's office situated at the front of the house in a room with a large window. Stu's old wood desk was gone, replaced by a black-and-white steel thing that looked as modern as the FortuneMedia sign.

It was much too easy imagining Reeve sitting behind it, wearing those black-rimmed glasses while he impatiently brushed the hair off his forehead...

She dropped the envelope on the glossy surface and hurried back downstairs and to her laptop.

This time when she opened a blank page, she didn't erase the sentences just as quickly as she wrote them.

The Chatelaine Report.

There be castles among us! At least one, anyway, and after hanging there for a while recently—no, it was NOT a honeymoon, but we'll talk about that later—this reporter learned the castle is a heartfelt homage to Chatelaine's mining history...

Chapter Ten

"For the love of Pete, Reeve. Can you at least put down your cell phone for a few minutes and look at the menu?"

Reeve dragged his attention from the screen on his phone to his sister sitting across the table from him. "Was just reading a blog."

Behind Gigi, the terrace that stretched nearly to the water's edge was already crowded. The wall of windows had been opened, allowing the evening breeze to drift through the Chef's Table dining room, stirring Gigi's long blond hair.

Or maybe that was caused by Harrison sitting beside her with his arm resting over the back of her chair.

It struck Reeve as protective.

Not a bad thing, in his estimation.

"What blog?" Gigi asked suspiciously.

Reeve slid his phone into his jacket pocket. *"The Chatelaine Report."* He'd been more than entertained by Isabel's humorous recounting of her sojourn at the castle. She'd relayed much of the same information that Smitty had droned on so endlessly about, but devoid of the yawn factor.

She'd also deferred discussing the reason she'd been hanging at the castle in the first place.

Which only made him wonder why. She'd had plenty of time to address the reasons why she had escaped the church without a new groom. Reeve had taken her home from the castle on Monday. Now it was Friday. He hadn't talked to her. Hadn't seen her, even though he'd spent the last day and a half at the Stellar building taking care of FortuneMedia business before heading back to the mining office that afternoon.

The official statement issued from the groom's quarter the day after the non-wedding had cryptically stated that the ceremony had been postponed due to a family emergency and followed it up with the standard request to please respect their need for privacy "at this difficult time."

No mention at all that the supposed emergency had been prompted by the groom getting caught on camera with a naked woman in his arms.

The social media post from Trey's bachelor party had since disappeared as if it had never been—suggesting that the Fitzgeralds' influence ran even deeper and wider than Reeve had thought. Like most things, though, what the Fitzgeralds had said officially dif-

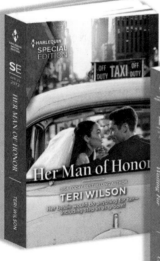

Get up to 4
FREE FABULOUS BOOKS
You Love!

To thank you for being a loyal reader we'd like to send you up to 4 FREE BOOKS, absolutely free when you try the Harlequin Reader Service.

Just write "YES" on the Loyal Reader Voucher and we'll send you 2 free books from each series you choose and a Free Mystery Gift, altogether worth over $20.

Try **Harlequin® Special Edition** and get 2 books featuring comfort and strength in the support of loved ones and enjoying the journey no matter what life throws your way.

Try **Harlequin® Heartwarming™ Larger-Print** and get 2 books featuring uplifting stories where the bonds of friendship, family and community unite.

Or **TRY BOTH and get 2 books from each series!**

Your free books are completely free, even the shipping! If you continue with your subscription, you can look forward to curated monthly shipments of brand-new books from your selected series, always at a discount off the cover price! Plus you can cancel any time.

So don't miss out, return your Loyal Readers Voucher today to get your Free books.

Pam Powers

LOYAL READER
FREE BOOKS VOUCHER

▲ If offer card is missing write to: Harlequin Reader Service, P.O. Box 1341, Buffalo, NY 14240-8531 or visit www.ReaderService.com ▲

BUSINESS REPLY MAIL
FIRST-CLASS MAIL   PERMIT NO. 717   BUFFALO, NY

POSTAGE WILL BE PAID BY ADDRESSEE

HARLEQUIN READER SERVICE
PO BOX 1341
BUFFALO NY 14240-8571

NO POSTAGE
NECESSARY
IF MAILED
IN THE
UNITED STATES

fered wildly from the commentary. Stories behind the bride's flight from the church had ranged from anxiety attacks to a bout of appendicitis to hush-hush addictions on the bride's part that the beleaguered groom could no longer tolerate.

"Making sure the blog isn't flouting the cease and desist?" Gigi asked him.

Reeve sighed faintly. "You know that I only threatened to file suit. I never actually did it."

Gigi rested her elbow delicately on the table and propped her pointed chin on her palm. "And why is that?"

He knew by her smug smile that she already thought she knew. She just wanted to hear him say it.

Fair enough. In the last several weeks, he'd learned a lot about his sister and what had motivated her—namely feeling cut out of the family business she claimed she'd wanted to run. He was willing to cut her some slack because of that, as well as his oblivious participation in the whole thing. She'd said that Walter had told her she could do anything—be anything—that she wanted. Including sitting at the top spot of Fortune Metals.

But Reeve knew one thing that Gigi did not.

She could coach people every day of the year about the importance of speaking up and leaning in. But she was nowhere near as cutthroat as he'd had to be in the wake of PJ's abbreviated tenure as CEO. And Reeve sincerely hoped she would never have to be.

"Because I was *wrong* to threaten it in the first place," he said, providing the answer she expected.

Her smile widened with sisterly satisfaction. She sat back and picked up her narrow, embossed menu. "I can't decide what I want," she said. "Harrison, what strikes your fancy?"

The attorney slid her a deliberate look. "It's not on the menu."

Reeve was surprised to see his sister actually blush. He hadn't thought she was capable of it.

He glanced around for their server, but he was busy with a large party on the terrace.

He picked up his empty glass and rattled the ice cubes. "I'm going up to the bar. Order me the rib eye if Joey gets over here before I'm back." He'd dined at the restaurant often enough to know the mainstays that were always on the menu regardless of the seasonal changeups.

Gigi and Harrison hardly seemed to notice when he left the table.

Love. It turned even a former JAG attorney like Harrison Vasquez into a marshmallow.

Reeve wondered how long it would be before their wedding. Knowing Gigi and what Reeve considered her needless preoccupation with her age of forty, it probably wouldn't be long. Then maybe his sister would finally have the babies that she'd always wanted.

He left the dining room and walked up a flight of stairs to the bar. The LC Club was typically crowded on a summer Friday night. He worked his way to the gleaming bar top and as soon as he did, one of the bartenders immediately approached. "Evening, Mr. Fortune. The usual?"

"On the rocks, please." He glanced around. Like the dining room below, the wall of windows here was pushed open and a crush of people were dancing on the balcony. Easily three-fourths of the women were wearing black. Short black. Long black. Tight black. Loose black.

Delphine was a big proponent of the little black dress.

Maybe that's why he smiled slightly when he saw a flash of vibrant yellow in the middle of the crowd.

A canary in the coal mine.

The bartender set Reeve's whiskey near his elbow. "On your tab?"

"Appreciate it." He tossed down some cash for a tip and took his drink back to the dining room, where his sister and Harrison had just finished giving their orders to Joey.

Reeve sat down across from them again and squinted over the rim of his glass at his sister. "What spurred this tête-à-tête, anyway? Come to ask me to pay for the wedding?" It was a facetious question. Gigi had plenty of her own money.

She was giving him a look. "The wedding is *not* the reason why I asked you to join us. But since you brought it up, we haven't quite decided on the date yet. When we do, though, I'd—" She exhaled before continuing in a rush. "I'd like you to give me away."

It was the last thing that Reeve expected and the sudden pressure in his chest was either emotion or the onset of a heart attack.

Since he'd come through his latest physical with

flying colors, he had to acknowledge it was more likely emotion. "I—" He cleared his throat. "I'll have Cora get it on my schedule."

Harrison just shook his head over the two of them.

Reeve knew that *his* family was far more normal than Reeve and Gigi's had ever been with parents who couldn't even remember their birthdays.

But Gigi was beaming at Reeve as if he'd admitted what he really meant. That he'd be honored.

He shifted in his chair and cleared his throat again. "Now that we've gotten that out of the way, what *is* the reason we're breaking bread together again?" It wasn't as if it were a usual occurrence for them, yet this was twice in the span of a month.

Gigi dabbed her finger to the corner of her eye and blinked a few times. Harrison squeezed her shoulder and drummed his fingers lightly on the white linen. "Mariana Sanchez wants to meet," he said bluntly. "And I think you should," he spoke over Reeve's equally blunt response.

Reeve washed the rest of his oath down with a sip of whiskey and looked from Harrison to Gigi. "It wasn't too long ago you thought we could pay her off for fifty grand."

"I was wrong."

Reeve caught yet another look passing between Gigi and Harrison and if he'd still been a kid, he'd have felt excluded all over again. But he was a lot older now. Maybe a little wiser. Certainly a lot harder.

"Gigi, you think it's a good idea?" he asked quietly. "Even though it's giving credence to the notion that *Grampy*—" he deliberately used her pet name for their great-grandfather "—wasn't perfect after all?"

Gigi flickered another glance at Harrison. "If what Mariana says is true, then I don't believe he ever knew. Look. I know I dismissed her claims from the get-go. I thought she was out to make a quick profit the same as you. But since then, Harrison has verified all the facts that she's put forward." Gigi folded her arms on the table and leaned forward. "Her mother was a woman named Maribel who'd been left at the foundling hospital in Rambling Rose when she was an infant. The only thing Maribel had was a pink blanket with a monogrammed F in one corner."

"A monogram is hardly—"

"Would you let me finish?"

He swallowed his impatience. He made a go-ahead swirl with his icy whiskey glass, watching the condensation dampen the white linen tablecloth.

She exhaled, obviously conquering her own impatience with him. "A couple by the name of Sanchez adopted her. Maribel died without ever telling Mariana about her true history." She shook her head slightly. "Maribel was obviously secretive. She raised Mariana on her own. Mariana has no idea who her own father was."

"She didn't begin suspecting her mother had been adopted at all until the last year or so," Harrison inserted.

"If Maribel was adopted, how does this lead to Grandfather?"

"Maribel's birth mother and Grampy were obviously involved at some point, and one thing led to another and—"

"Baby booties," Reeve finished. He briefly pinched the bridge of his nose.

"The foundling hospital was closed decades ago," Gigi went on. "Eventually the building came down as well and a children's clinic went up in its place. The original records have been long gone, so Mariana thought she was at a dead end figuring out exactly what her connection was to the Fortunes."

Harrison nodded. "Until Martin Smith showed up last year and shed some light on things."

Reeve frowned at the lawyer. "Who the hell is Martin Smith?"

"Wendell Fortune's best friend. He's the one who connected the dots for Mariana."

Reeve immediately shook his head. "Doesn't wash." If Wendell had had a best friend, Walter would have known about it and there'd have been at least *some* mention of him in his journals.

Not if their friendship happened during the missing years.

He ignored the whispered logic inside his head. It sounded too similar to Isabel's voice.

Gigi spread her hands, looking frustrated. "Harrison says that this Mr. Smith knows all the details about Wendell. The time he spent in Europe and India. His death."

Reeve looked at Harrison again. "You talked to him yourself?"

"He has a residence in Rambling Rose, and I've

been trying to reach him, but so far, we've missed each other. I know he's had some health problems over the last few years, but he still travels a fair amount." Harrison lifted his fingertips, calmly forestalling Reeve. "I *have* spoken personally with Mariana though. More than once. And corroborated her statements enough with others to be satisfied she's on the level. She said that Martin often talks about Wendell's belief that being a Fortune had ruined his life. And by extension, that he hadn't wanted his descendants' lives also ruined. Which is why he was never involved in their lives. But at the end of the day, with Wendell long gone, Martin felt compelled to reveal the truth."

Reeve latched onto the point. "The truth about *Wendell's* grandchildren. Doesn't mean Mariana has a claim on Walter's estate."

Harrison shook his head. "Martin says she's Walter's. And the DNA at least backs up that possibility."

"What about Edgar or Elias?" Reeve wasn't ready to let that possibility go. "Either one of them is just as likely a source as Walter." Reeve hadn't even known they'd existed until they'd been mentioned practically on the first page of Walter's final journal—as if he'd been picking right up from whatever he'd been recounting in the prior volume.

Reeve hadn't been sure he'd been reading Walter's spindly writing correctly. He'd had Cora pull old birth records to confirm he wasn't mistaken before he'd even told Gigi about their existence.

Meanwhile, his sister was looking thunderstruck.

"I hadn't thought about them!" She looked at Harrison. "They're Walter's half brothers, too, just like Wendell!"

"And a lot more mysterious," Harrison said. "If it weren't for the information Reeve gave me a few weeks ago, it would be like they'd never existed."

A lot like Trey's bachelor party pictures, Reeve thought.

"I haven't been able to trace their whereabouts after the mining accident any further than Colima in Mexico. But in any case, Martin's the one who pointed Mariana in Walter's direction," Harrison said. "Even before we learned that Wendell had two other brothers."

"Martin's in on the scam."

Gigi shook her head. "It's feeling less and less like a scam, Reeve. Martin had to hire a private investigator to track down Wendell's descendants. In the process of that, he found Mariana as well."

"All right, then. If we take it as true—" he lifted his hand "—and I'm not saying that I do, then who is Maribel's birth mother? Did Martin Smith give her that information?"

"A woman named Luz Cortez," Harrison provided. "Is the name familiar at all?"

Reeve shook his head. So did Gigi.

Joey arrived then with their salads and disappeared after efficiently serving them all.

Harrison was the only one to pick up his fork and stab it into his Caesar's.

"You said Wendell's descendants," Reeve repeated.

"Plural. How many? And how much is it going to cost us?"

"Four brothers and a sister," Harrison said.

Gigi tucked her hair behind her ear and the diamond and ruby ring on her finger winked. "The Maloneys live in Chatelaine. Well, the sister is in Rambling Rose. And it isn't costing *us* anything." A faint line appeared between Gigi's eyebrows. "I thought you'd been reading Isabel's blog about it. She's been covering it for months. How a few of the Chatelaine locals were suddenly becoming rich after learning they were Wendell Fortune's grandchildren."

Reeve absorbed that. "Months?" he said carefully.

"Well…" Gigi spread her hands helplessly. "Yes."

The only entry that he'd read in its entirety was the one still opened on his phone about the castle. He hadn't even made it all the way through the one Isabel had written about Mariana Sanchez, because he'd been too busy seeing red.

And he was starting to see that shade all over again.

Why hadn't Isabel mentioned what she'd known about Wendell when she'd been at the castle? She'd had ample time and she hadn't uttered one damn word.

Trust or rope, he thought grimly.

She'd chosen the rope.

"Obviously, I haven't been reading them," he said evenly. "So get me up to speed now."

Gigi sighed noisily, as if frustrated by his attitude and Harrison calmly covered her fist on top of the table with his palm. "The investigator Martin hired was supposed to find a child that Wendell suspected had been born to a woman named Marjorie Maloney," he said. "They'd been briefly involved when Wendell was a young man, but for whatever reason, the relationship didn't work out and he ended up going to Europe. According to Martin, Wendell regretted never knowing for sure if Marjorie had been pregnant or not. Particularly toward the end of his life."

"Maybe Wendell should have stuck around to find out for himself, then," Reeve said flatly. "Instead of jaunting around the world collecting architectural tips about castles."

What had been Walter's excuse where his own failings were concerned?

"There's no point in judging Wendell all of these years after the fact," Gigi said briskly. "What's done is done. Meanwhile, the investigator did confirm there'd been a child named Rick Maloney. His mother never married, though it sounds like there were plenty of men who came and went. Rick married young, had several kids only to leave his wife while she'd been pregnant with their last—"

"Prince of a guy," Harrison inserted. "Carrying on the family tradi—" He broke off and gave Reeve a chagrined look. "Sorry."

Reeve ignored it. Harrison wasn't thinking anything that Reeve himself wasn't.

As if uninterrupted, Gigi continued. "Then Rick married a second time—no kids resulted this time—but he apparently died in a motorcycle wreck. Which left those children from his first marriage as Wendell's only heirs. Martin has been working ever since to bestow on them the inheritance that he says Wendell once talked about. These people have gone from being ordinary Joes and Josephines—"

"Justine," Harrison said. "The granddaughter's name is Justine."

Gigi barely missed a beat. "And her brothers are Linc, Max, Cooper and Damon," she reeled off. "My point is their modest beginnings have been significantly altered as a result of their inheritances."

"I don't know what kind of game this Smith guy is playing or whose money he's bestowing," Reeve said through his teeth. "Because all of Wendell's assets, including the castle, went into the Fortune Trust when he died."

Gigi looked confused. "That doesn't make sense. If the money's not coming from Wendell's estate, where is it coming from?"

"Guess we can add figuring that out on top of verifying whether Edgar and Elias Fortune produced any heirs that are going to come out of the woodwork when we least expect it. That whole side of Walter's family is turning into nothing but trouble."

"Reeve," Gigi chided. "That's harsh, even for you."

"Separating the wheat from the chaff is always necessary, Gigi. I learned that from our great-grandfather. You should have, too." He flagged down Joey. "Cancel the steak if you can. I won't be staying. And if it's too late, tell the chef to take it home for his dog."

The server immediately headed off.

Gigi caught Reeve's hand. "I didn't intend to upset you."

He squeezed her fingers. "I know." He exhaled. "I'm not upset with you." He wasn't even upset with Isabel, exactly. She'd done what she'd been doing all along—collecting gossip about his family so she could turn it into a revenue stream.

Upset with himself? That was another story.

He should have known better. People never changed their stripes. Not even brown-eyed brunettes with the ability to tie him into knots.

"Then what do we do about Mariana Sanchez?" Gigi was looking at him expectantly. "Regardless of what's going on with Wendell, we still have to deal with her."

"Double the payoff," he said abruptly.

His sister and Harrison shared another look. "It won't work," they said in unison.

"Then triple it and if she still doesn't bite, I'll start considering a countersuit."

"For *what*?" Gigi exclaimed. "As Harrison has pointed out to me *many* times, Mariana hasn't initiated any legal actions."

"It's a matter of time." Reeve was certain of it.

Harrison was shaking his head. "Trying to buy her off is the wrong move, Reeve. The recognition Mariana wants is not through money and the longer this goes on, the more insistent she'll get. So far, the only media attention has been in *The Chatelaine Re-*

port, which is seriously small potatoes. It could go a lot further and you'll end up with a PR nightmare."

Reeve shot back the rest of his whiskey and thumped the empty glass down on the table. "We'll see. Just do it."

Then he walked out of the restaurant while he still had his temper in hand.

He strode through the building and went out through one of the rear entrances that only the staff used. He could remember when it had once been Walter's service entrance.

He walked through the congestion of employee cars parked there and made his way around to the paved shoreline walk. He could hear laughter and music from the balconies behind him. Voices and conversations from the narrow strip of sand between the walkway and the soft lap of water.

It was a warm summer night and the lure of the lake had brought people out in droves.

Had he really believed that he could trust Isabel even after she'd admitted she was the author behind *The Chatelaine Report*? What a convenient serendipity for her that she'd run into him on the church steps.

A method to escape her wedding *and* a bonanza of family information that Reeve had been all too willing to share.

All because he'd wanted to believe the look in those wide eyes of hers had been sincere.

He pulled out his cell phone where Isabel's castle blog was still displayed.

He didn't even realize he'd stopped on the sidewalk until he heard a "whoa, dude," behind him and a skateboarder flew around him, missing him by inches.

He grimaced and pocketed the phone again, glancing back at the LC Club. A fire was burning in the firepit down by the water. He imagined he could still see Gigi and Harrison sitting at their table. On the balcony above them, he saw that flash of canary yellow still moving among the other dancers.

On the balcony above that, the pace was a little slower. People sitting around on deeply cushioned outdoor furniture beneath the flickering lights from dozens of hanging lanterns.

Despite being just a short distance from his condo, he reversed direction, walking back toward the LC Club again. He bypassed the first floor altogether and went straight up to the second-floor bar. He ordered another drink and carried it out to the balcony, slowly making his way to the railing that looked out over the shoreline walk.

He leaned on the rail and sipped his drink, staring at the moon's rippling reflection on the water.

Walter. Who'd seemed to value family over all unless their names happened to be Edgar and Elias. And Wendell, who hadn't valued anyone until it was too late. What kind of men had they really been?

A woman wearing a black bikini top and a high-waisted black skirt stopped next to him, interrupting his thoughts. "You look lonely."

"I'm not."

She pushed out her lower lip, shining with bright red lipstick. "Oh, now, don't be shy. Come and dance." She held out her hand and waggled her fingertips in invitation.

"I'm not shy. And I'm not interested. But don't take it personally." He wryly tipped his glass in acknowledgment. "I give you credit for your confidence."

Her teeth were very white as she smiled. "Honey, I'm confident about all sorts of things." She hung her arms over the top of the railing the same as he, giving him an eye-popping view of cleavage. "I'm Lola. And you are...?"

She clearly was not going to go away.

He lifted his glass again. The ice was melting fast, watering down the whiskey. "Reeve," he finally offered.

"Haven't seen you around here before, Reeve."

Then she hadn't looked since he'd been stopping in there almost weekly ever since he'd bought his place on the lake.

Resigned, he turned his back on the moonlit water. "What about you? You live around here?"

She nodded. "East shore." She waved a languid hand as if to indicate the location. "You?"

He barely even heard her. The flash of yellow that had been in the middle of the crowd of dancers had separated itself and was storming toward the door, glossy brown hair bouncing around her shoulders.

Isabel.

The sight of her was like a punch in the gut.

How had he not realized it was her earlier?

"Excuse me, Lola." He didn't even glance at her as he headed toward the door, too, but someone else was ahead of him.

Trey Fitzgerald, who was following hard in Isabel's wake.

Reeve stopped short. Right. How could he forget?

He shoved his fingers through his hair and turned on his heel again.

Lola was across the balcony, smiling at him. A bird in hand, he thought wearily.

He pushed a smile to his lips and headed her way.

Chapter Eleven

Isabel jabbed the elevator button and when it didn't immediately open, she started for the wide staircase.

She was furious. With Seanmarie for one. With herself for another. She hadn't wanted to go out for drinks, but Seanmarie had been bugging her all week because she'd been given a gift certificate to the LC Club from her parents that was nearly expired.

You're the only single friend I have left, Isabel. Please come with me. Then I won't have to lie to my mom when she asks for the millionth time if I'm ever getting out of the house.

At first, things had been fine. Seanmarie had wanted to meet at the LC Club even though it would have been simpler for them to drive out to the lake together. But Isabel hadn't argued. They'd met up as planned. They'd had a drink. They'd joined the crush of people dancing just for the sake of dancing.

And then Trey had appeared.

And Seanmarie had disappeared.

If not for that fact, Isabel *might* have believed it was a coincidence.

She closed her hand over the banister and started down the stairs, moving as fast as her wedge sandals allowed.

"Princess, hold up."

She gritted her teeth and rounded on him. "I am *not* your princess, and I can almost guarantee that *no* grown woman appreciates being called that by any man except maybe her father. How'd you do it, anyway? Get to Seanmarie? Convince her to collude with you to get me here?"

"She doesn't matter." Trey spread his hands, doing his best impression of looking conciliatory.

"Doesn't matter?" Isabel raised her eyebrows. "That's the problem with you, Trey. Thinking that using people doesn't matter! Thinking that loyalty and...and commitment are just convenient shirts to pull on and off whenever it suits you!"

His lips thinned but he managed a smile when a trio of woman came skipping down the staircase. "Evening, ladies."

Evening! They twittered in unison and kept going.

Isabel could hear a whispered, giggly "TFIII" as they passed her.

She huffed out a breath and took another step, but

Trey latched his fingers around her wrist, stopping her. "Pri—Isabel. *Wait*."

"Don't touch me," she said coolly, and stared him in the face until he flushed a little and released her wrist.

As soon as he did, she started down the stairs again. She had a strong desire to find a restroom and wash her hand up to her armpit.

"You wouldn't be this upset if you weren't still in love with me," he said, following closely.

She didn't bother looking at him. "I'm not upset with you, Trey. You're who you are. My mistake was having expectations that you could *never* live up to. Like at least being faithful through the wedding day. The person I'm most furious with is myself for wasting as much time on you as I did!"

She stopped short and turned on him again, poking her finger into his surprised face. "I was even foolish enough to feel guilty for the way I called it off. Running out like that in such a public way. I worried about the embarrassment I might have caused you and your family. But you know what?" She raised her hands and dropped them. "I don't even care about *that* anymore. Thanks to you, I have friends calling to see how I'm doing in *rehab*! If there's anyone who should be ashamed or embarrassed, it's you. But you're never going to be ashamed of anything, because you're TFIII. Texas's gift to the world."

She snorted softly and eyed him up and down, from black wavy hair to designer tennis shoes that would be tossed aside at the first scuff mark. "I am *not* in love with you, Trey. Not anymore. So stop leaving me voice mails. Stop texting. Stop manipulating my friends and my coworkers to help you. I will *never* come back to you. I will never marry you. Is *that* clear enough for you?" She waited, but all he did was force another smile when the same three twittering girls came skipping back up the stairs again.

She exhaled. "I will pick up my stuff from your house tomorrow afternoon. Four o'clock," she added, plucking the time out of thin air just so he couldn't claim that she'd been unspecific. "For both of our sakes, *do not be there*!"

Then she turned her back on him and went down the rest of the stairs and headed for the nearest exit.

She'd left her car in the parking lot, but it was blocked in by a pickup truck the size of a small semi. "Just...perfect."

She pulled her cell phone out of the hidden pocket on the side of her dress and sent a text message to Seanmarie. Really?

Seanmarie's response was immediate, as if she'd been waiting. He's the perfect guy!

Isabel grimaced. Then YOU marry him. She sent it and pocketed the phone again. She had no desire to stand around waiting for the owner of the supersized truck to appear and no desire to go back into the LC Club.

Instead, her head of steam fueled her all the way around the enormous club. Somewhere along the way, she started trying to figure out which part of it might have been Walter and Effie's home. But she couldn't see any differences in stucco and stone or the various levels of terracing or red slate roof tiles.

By the time she reached the shoreline walk, the worst of her irritation with Trey had faded.

The pizzeria sign was to her right. Which made her think of Reeve. She hadn't heard from him all week.

Not that she'd expected to.

But when she'd dropped by the office earlier that day to use the internet again, the envelope she'd left on his desk had been gone.

She turned the opposite direction and walked a while. Long enough for the noise and music from the LC Club to soften. Long enough for the crowds to thin. She smiled at the young couple pushing a stroller. At the gray-haired couple walking leisurely hand in hand. At the teenagers on roller skates weaving in and out of everyone they passed.

She'd wanted all of that. The stroller. The kids. A man to hold her hand.

She still did.

But not with a man like Trey.

She stepped off the sidewalk when a bicyclist sped past. The soles of her shoes immediately sank into the sand, and she reached down to slip them off. Then she curled her toes and inhaled deeply. Warm evening air scented by cool rippling water drifted through her hair and fluttered her yellow dress. It filled her lungs and cleared her mind.

Today is the first day of the rest of your life.

The saying was old. Trite. But true, nevertheless.

Dangling her shoes from her fingers, she wandered across the sand to sit on an empty bench facing the water.

She stretched out her feet and stared across the water, wondering which direction Wendell's Folly lay.

"Where's lover boy?"

She jerked and swung around to see Reeve. His suit coat was bunched in his hand, his tie pulled loose, and his white shirtsleeves rolled up his forearms.

And all the calm that she'd felt after telling off Trey once and for all fluttered away on a breathless breeze. "Reeve." She curled her fingers around the edge of the cement bench. "What're you doing here?"

"I have a condo here, remember? Same as your fiancé."

"He's not my fiancé and, strictly speaking, he has a house." It was dark out, but there was plenty of light. The sky was clear, the moon bright. Add in the simulated tiki torches that bordered the shoreline walk and she had no trouble at all seeing the expression on Reeve's face. "What's wrong?"

"Why didn't you mention Martin Smith?"

She frowned. "Who?"

"Martin Smith," he enunciated as if she were dim.

She pushed off the bench. "I don't know anyone by that name. Why?"

"He's been spreading money around supposedly in Wendell Fortune's name. You've blogged about it. So don't lie—"

"Hold on." She lifted her hand. "Don't accuse me

of lying. Or of libel or anything else in that vein. Been there. Done that, remember?"

She could see a muscle flexing in his jaw. Then he pulled his cell phone out of his pants pocket, and he swiped the screen a few times. "This is from *The Chatelaine Report.*" He quoted, "'No one would have guessed that GreatStore manager Linc Maloney would turn out to be the mastermind behind last month's Lake Chatelaine New Year's bash. Now we have learned that his true name is Linc *Fortune* Maloney,'" he practically spit the name, "'and he is suddenly a very rich man.' Yada yada." He pointed his phone at her. "These Maloney people are connected to Mariana Sanchez, and you knew it."

"I told you I learned about Mariana from another source and that I went to *her* to get her story. Was I supposed to tell you that source was *Linc*? And what's that got to do with this Martin person, anyway?"

"He's the one doling out money to them supposedly in Wendell's name!"

She blinked. "So? I never even thought about Wendell until you took me to the castle. All I knew then was that some rich guy was leaving bequests to his grandsons who happened to be some of Chatelaine's own. *That's* what I wrote about. Linc throwing a New Year's party. Max getting bought at a Valentine auction. I never once wrote about the source of their sudden windfalls or tried to draw a connection to you until I met their cousin, Mariana!"

He snorted derisively and it made her nerves fizz unpleasantly. But she kept her temper. "*Their* grandfather was acknowledging them from beyond the grave, yet Mariana couldn't get the time of day out of you or Gigi!" She lifted her hands. "I wrote about *that* because it was interesting! And why would this Martin guy be giving away money in Wendell's name if it weren't really Wendell's?" She waited. "Well?"

He exhaled sharply and rubbed his hand down his face. "What were you doing, dancing with Trey?"

She was going to get whiplash at the rate he was going. "I wasn't!"

"I saw you."

"Really?" She stomped across the sand until she was mere inches from him. "You saw me *dance* with Trey? You sure about that, Mr. Fortune?"

The muscle in his jaw flexed.

"You know what you do?" She jabbed her finger against his unforgivingly hard chest. "You see a few details and make sweeping judgments based on things that aren't remotely related. You won't talk to Mariana because of the Agnoli thing. You read some journals that don't even cover *half* of your great-grandfather's life and think you know everything there is to know about him and his brother. You see me in the same place as Trey and assume I've fallen meekly right back into his arms!" She tossed up her arms again. "You know what? It doesn't matter what you think. Fire me. Close down my blog. I'm a writer. I'll find a way to write that doesn't have one damn thing to do with *you*."

She snatched up her shoes and headed back toward

the LC Club, her footsteps nowhere near as fast as she'd have liked, thanks to the shifting sand. If that stupid truck still had her blocked in, she'd call a rideshare to take her home.

"You're right."

She pretended not to hear. Mostly because she was pretty sure it was only her wishful thinking.

"Issa."

She closed her eyes. "The only ones who get to call me that are people who love me." Dammit, that didn't sound right at all. "I mean my *family*." And he'd have only known it was her nickname because he'd seen the text message she'd sent from his phone the night of the wedding.

"Okay. You're right. I…made assumptions." The admission sounded like it made him want to choke. "It's something my sister has accused me of doing lately, too."

Her shoulders sagged. She so didn't have the energy to have her feelings tangled up this way. She knew she'd done the right thing where Trey was concerned. But that was the only thing she knew. When it came to Reeve…?

"Come and have a drink with me," he said.

She opened her eyes. The LC Club gleamed bright and busy ahead of her.

"Anywhere but the LC Club," she said.

"Done."

She slowly turned to face him. He was holding out his hand.

"Nothing's going to happen but a drink," she

warned. Then flushed because it was a mighty bold assumption on her own part to think he might have meant anything else.

His hand didn't waver. "It's too soon," he said. "I know."

She chewed the inside of her cheek. "What're we going to talk about?"

"We don't have to talk about anything."

She extended her hand toward his. "Fine." But instead of giving him her hand, she looped her sandals over his fingers.

Then she balled her hands safely inside her dress pockets. She curled her toes into the sand again. "Where to?"

"Right over there." He pointed toward the shoreline walk.

The only thing she saw was Snowman's Creamery. A milkshake wasn't her immediate idea of a "drink," but it was probably a safer one. She began walking, which on a thick bed of sand was never all that graceful. Trying to do it brusquely was outright impossible.

When they reached the cement walkway, she stopped and brushed the sand from her feet and reached for her shoes.

He handed them to her. "But you don't really need 'em." His lips quirked. "Bare being better."

A swath of heat cut through her like a knife through soft butter. "I'm not worried about falling here," she said as she pushed her feet into the wedges. At least they weren't as complicated as her wedding sandals had been.

There were tables and chairs outside the creamery, and she crossed the walkway, angling toward them. Reeve, however, angled away from them.

"Over here," he said.

She changed course and followed him beyond the bright lights of the ice cream shop and through a tall gate surrounded on both sides by equally tall bushes. The deep wooden deck on the other side wasn't entirely different from one of the decks at the LC Club. Only it was unoccupied. And attached to what was obviously a home.

Modern lines. Lots of glass. Lots of wood and metal.

He'd called it a condo. She should have known better than to think that meant small and unassuming.

She thought she did a good job of not gulping outright, but her brain imitated one anyway. Her mouth followed the signals, going immediately dry.

She swallowed and moistened her lips.

"Something wrong?"

She shook her head. "No." What could possibly be wrong?

He crossed to a thick pillar and hit a switch. Warm golden light suddenly glowed upward from the corners of the deck, marking the perimeter as efficiently as the cable-style railing did. He went up the few steps and tossed his jacket carelessly onto a long all-weather dining table surrounded by a half dozen chairs. The deck was also large enough for a thickly cushioned couch and several chairs.

"Make yourself comfortable." He pressed his hand against a module next to the sliding doors and one of the glass panels glided open.

He disappeared into the dark interior.

She turned away and exhaled carefully. One drink, she promised herself. That was it. Then she'd go.

By the time he returned several minutes later, she'd arranged herself in one of the cushioned chairs across from the couch, her feet tucked underneath her.

He handed her a glass of wine. "More assumptions on my part. Hopefully forgivable in this case."

She took the stemmed glass from him, careful not to brush his fingers with her own. "It is. Thank you." She took a sip. The chardonnay was exactly the kind she liked. Rich and buttery and heady.

He sat down on the couch opposite her and twisted off the top of a longneck bottle of beer. Then he stretched across the divide between them. "Cheers."

She leaned forward and lightly tapped her glass against his bottle. "Cheers."

They both sat back. He took a pull from his bottle, then stretched out his long legs, crossing them at the ankle. Then he leaned his head back against his seat cushion and exhaled deeply.

He'd said they didn't have to talk about anything.

Apparently, he'd meant it.

She couldn't quite decide if she found the silence nerve-racking or not. Halfway through her glass of wine, she decided it wasn't.

She rested the base of her glass on the wide arm

of her chair and stared out at the water. "I don't know how you stand such an appalling view," she finally murmured.

"Great strength of will."

She smiled faintly and pointed to a narrow boat, sails furled, bobbing gently alongside a dock that was nearly directly ahead of his house. "Is that yours?"

"Neighbor's."

She looked over her shoulder. His deck was completely surrounded on both sides by trees and tall shrubs. Only the lakefront side was open straight out to the water. Not only was the ice cream parlor invisible from where they sat, so was whatever kind of condo his neighbor occupied on the other side.

She rested her chin on her arm. "You should probably sail more often. It would help your stress level."

"Who says I'm stressed?"

She smiled faintly. "It's about eleven o'clock on a Friday night and you're wearing a *suit*. If you're not stressed, you ought to be."

In answer, he pulled off his tie and pitched it at her. It landed unerringly on her lap.

She draped it over the arm of her chair. "Do you like running two companies?"

"Yes."

"Really?

He waited a beat. "They're different."

"I don't know. I think it would be like having two wives."

He laughed softly. "*That* is a comparison I have never heard." He swirled the base of his beer bottle in

a slow circle. "I have more freedom with FortuneMedia. And a deep responsibility for Fortune Metals."

"Spoken like a good great-grandson." She smoothed
her thumb crosswise over the tie. It was dark with a
subtle dot pattern.

"A lot of people depend on us for their livelihoods,"
he said. "Not just here in Texas. We have mining op-
erations in Arizona, Nevada, Utah, Michigan, Illi-
nois. A few others. Want me to get you the company
press kit?"

"And it all started from the silver mine in Chatelaine."

He smiled faintly. "Go back before Walter's time and
we've been into investments and banking, too. Walter's
father, Jensen Fortune, was an ambitious man."

"I'd say the gene has stayed strong." She realized
she was studying the narrow wedge of skin showing
above the two unfastened buttons at Reeve's neck and
turned her gaze back out toward the water. "Which
way is the castle from here?"

He got up from the couch and crouched beside her
chair. His arm stretched over her shoulder as if he
were lining up a rifle sight. "If it were light out, you'd
be able to just make out the towers through the trees."

All she could do was stare blindly into the distance. The trees were nothing but shapes and shadows beneath the moonlight.

But the scent of him—oh, that delicious scent of
him—was permeating her cells with exquisite clar-
ity. And his warmth was making something inside
her shiver.

She swallowed her last gulp of wine, which left

her with nothing to do but strangle the glass between her hands.

When she felt his fingertips sift through the ends of her hair, she melted a little. "Reeve."

"You're going to let me call you Issa one of these days," he murmured.

No. She melted a lot.

She turned her head until she could see him from the corner of her eye. If she turned any more, she was afraid she'd fall right into the magnetic pulse of him. It had taken Trey months to get her into bed, because she hadn't wanted to be just one more of his frequent conquests. But she was desperately aware that Reeve wouldn't have to work nearly as hard. "I think I should go."

His fingertips grazed her ear as he slowly tucked her hair behind it. "Probably a good idea."

She swallowed again and turned her head another inch. His gaze dropped and she knew instinctively that he was looking at her mouth.

When she realized she was starting to tip his way, she abruptly went boneless and slid underneath his arm, yanking her dress down around her thighs when it rode so far up to nearly show off her polka-dot panties. Soon as she cleared his arm, she popped to her feet like a bouncing ball.

She realized she was still clutching the empty wineglass and quickly went over to set it on the table where he'd thrown his suit coat.

He stood more slowly. "You have a car?"

She nodded quickly. "At the LC Club."

"I'll walk you back."

"No!" She backed toward the steps. "I mean that's not necessary. It's perfectly safe. There are tons of people."

"Isabel. I'll *walk* you back."

She held up her hand, staving him off. "The only thing I need protection from right now is you. Us." She waved her index finger back and forth between them. "This. So please. Just stay here. I'll be fine." She pulled her cell phone out of her pocket. "Trusty phone. Fully charged."

"Then use it and call me when you get to your car."

She nodded jerkily and fled.

Her shoes weren't exactly made for running, but she jogged all the way back to the LC Club as if a hungry dog was nipping at her heels.

Mercifully, the gargantuan truck was gone. She threw herself behind the wheel of her car and started the engine. Then she dialed Reeve's number.

He'd only written down his phone number that one time at the castle, but it felt forever etched in her brain.

"I'm here," she said when the ringing stopped. She couldn't help that she sounded breathless. She was. And not just from the jog. "Safe and sound."

"Thank you. Be careful driving back to town. The road's dark."

"I'm always careful," she said blithely.

Even though she hadn't been careful with him. At all.

Chapter Twelve

"This came by messenger for you." Cora handed Reeve a manila envelope. "It's that key you wanted." His executive assistant had an old-school appointment book in her hands. "I've rescheduled your appointment with Murphy from R&D, so you'll have time to stop in at Horvath's retirement party. His wife will be there." She tapped the eraser end of her pencil against her book. "Make sure you remember her name is Sheree, not Sherry. Sherry's his *ex*-wife. Got that? Sheree, Sheree, Sheree."

"Sheree," he repeated absently.

She nodded. "Your flight to Phoenix leaves at nine, so you'll have a legitimate excuse to toast and run. Frankly, I don't understand why you insisted on commercial when we have a perfectly good—" She fixed him with a beady eye over the rim of her glasses. "Are you listening?"

He turned the key over in his palm and wondered if he'd miss climbing through a window. "I always listen to you, Cora."

She made a disbelieving *hmmm*. She was seventy-nine years old and had worked for Walter, Philip Sr. and PJ. To her, Reeve was just one in a long line of Fortune Metals CEOs. She'd never married, and in Reeve's estimation, she worked even longer hours than he did despite his efforts to get her to scale back. To which her response was always that she'd scale back when she was dead.

"The updates to your calendar have been synced to all of your devices, so don't forget your phone."

"Do I ever forget my phone?" He gave her a look that was totally outdone by the one she gave back to him.

She bounced her pencil eraser again. "You'll have your usual suite at the Biltmore. You'll meet with the local execs tomorrow at ten, tour the new building and fly out again at two p.m. You'll be home in your jammies by seven." She closed her appointment book with a snap and tucked it beneath her skinny arm. "Anything you want me to take care of while you're gone?"

"Make sure the press release goes out about Gigi's seat on the board."

She looked pitying. "Challenge me a little, would you please?"

He rocked back in his chair. "You worked for Walter. Ever hear him talk about someone named Luz Cortez?"

Her expression softened the way it always did when the topic of his great-grandfather came up. "Cortez feels a little familiar. But not Luz Cortez."

"See what you can dig up. While you're at it, get together a full accounting of the Fortune Trust."

"You want the most recent audit, or—"

The audit was a year ago. "This isn't for the auditors. Just let me know if anything strikes you as odd."

Her eyes narrowed suspiciously. "Why?"

"Cora, just—" He exhaled. "PJ's been contacting me lately. I want to know if he's somehow managed to siphon off excess funds again. And keep it between us."

She looked at him over her glasses again. "Everything you say to me stays between us."

He raised his hands peaceably. Cora knew more about Fortune Metals than anyone and she was merciless if you got on her wrong side. She still detested PJ for what she considered his defection. She knew exactly what Reeve's father was capable of. "I don't know what I was thinking," he said wryly.

She gave her iconic *hmmm* again and left his office, closing the door after herself.

He tossed down the key and pushed out of his chair. His office was on the top floor of the Fortune Metals tower in Corpus Christi. The position of his desk—facing out the windows—was the only thing he hadn't changed when he'd become the CEO. Otherwise, he'd gotten rid of everything that smacked of

PJ. Where there'd once been claustrophobically dark paneling and elaborate heavy furnishings, now it was open. Clean lines. Gray juxtaposed with off-white.

Cora called it minimalist.

Reeve called it PJ-free.

He stood in front of the glass panes feeling almost surrounded by the sky. Directly below was the grassy, landscaped campus enjoyed by employees and shoppers alike. Directly out were the glittering waters of the bay.

He pulled out his cell phone and dialed Isabel.

"Gossips are us," she answered after the second ring. Her voice was bright. He could hear her smile.

He wondered if she'd been reliving those moments on his deck the same way he'd been. She'd never know how difficult it had been not to call her the next morning. Or the next. Sooner or later, it wouldn't be "too soon," and he didn't want to blow it because he was impatient.

"Let's go sailing," he said.

"Um…it's nine a.m. on a Monday morning. Don't you have to work for a living?"

He leaned his shoulder against the window and smiled. "I've been at my office for two hours."

"Madness. I haven't even had my coffee yet."

"Are you one of those types who don't roll out of bed until noon, then fire up your computer and work in your pajamas?"

"If I am, are you going to retract the sailing invitation?"

He chuckled, then felt his nerve-endings sizzle at

the sounds of rustling. It was intensely easy imagining her in her bed. "What *are* you doing?" Why not torture himself a little bit more?

"Unpacking a box of china that I inherited from my granny Sophia. I retrieved all my stuff from Trey's place this weekend. Along with a daunting array of wedding gifts to return. Which leaves me in a mountain of tissue paper and packing peanuts at the moment. And back to your question, no, I am not the remote-working jammie type. Well," she said consideringly, "I do work from home a lot. But not in my pajamas."

Any sort of pajama talk with Isabel was a trip down a road paved with cold showers. "Trey give you any grief picking up your stuff?"

She sighed faintly. He heard another rustle and a soft clink and imagined her carefully placing her granny's dishes on a shelf. "Not exactly. He wasn't even there. But his lawyer was. I gave him my door key and the ring, and in turn, he handed me an invoice lining out all the wedding expenses that Trey and his family now expect me to pay."

"You've got to be kidding me."

"Wish I were." She still sounded bright, but the smile was gone from her voice. "I mean they must know there's no way I can afford to pay it. The flowers alone cost more than a month of my salary. And that wedding stylist that I didn't even want in the first place? Oh, don't get me started." Without hesitation, she added, "Sailing when?"

Any time. Anywhere. "Saturday." He'd been thinking Lake Chatelaine, but the possibility of running into Trey was a real thing. "Here in Corpus Christi, if you don't mind driving over."

"Actually, that works really well, because I could stop in and see my folks."

"What time can you get here?"

"The very question makes me feel lazy. What time do you want to get out on your boat?"

"Early. By eight."

She gave a laughing groan. "You really do want to drag me out of bed early, don't you?"

"Honey, I'm not touching that with a ten-foot pole."

She laughed again and ended the call.

He was still smiling when Cora came in a few minutes later.

"You don't have time to stare mindlessly out the window. That's why you need curtains to cover them up." She moved a stack of folders from the cart she'd pushed them in on to his desk. "Contracts," she said briskly and left the office again.

He sighed faintly, returned to his desk and pulled out a pen to start signing them. Halfway through, he got up and opened his door. Cora was sitting at her desk outside his office, her fingers flying on her computer keyboard. "When's that political fundraising thing for Trace Fitzgerald?"

She didn't miss a keystroke. "Don't tell me you've changed your mind and want to go now. Your schedule—"

"I don't." He cut her off before she could get a full

head of steam going. "I want to pull the company's support for his campaign."

That surprised her enough to stop typing. She looked up at him. "The event is Wednesday," she finally said. "Fitzgerald getting into office is advantageous to mining in general. Why—"

"Because I don't like the way they operate," he said flatly.

She flipped open her calendar and made a note. "I'll get hold of his campaign manager and break the news today."

"If you get any pushback, let me know." He closed the door and returned to his desk and the pages that Cora had marked with little red flags that said, "sign here." He'd barely finished when she reminded him about a meeting he needed to attend across town. That was followed by another and another. Then it was Horvath's retirement party with his wife Sherry— Reeve remembered it was *Sheree* just in time—and then his car took him to the airport.

"Don't forget your bag, Mr. Fortune." The driver was young. New. She wore the usual white shirt and silver Fortune Metals tie that all the drivers wore. Her hand trembled ever so slightly when she extended his garment bag.

"Call me Reeve, Teresa."

She tucked her hands behind her back and bobbed her head. "Yes, sir."

"Did Cora have you pack it?"

She looked uncomfortable but she nodded. "Yes, sir."

Packing for Reeve typically meant picking up his suits and shirts from the cleaners located right at the campus of Fortune Metals. Only occasionally did it mean picking up something more personal from his home. Like his familiar garment bag.

"Thank you," he said, doing his best to remember the litany of accusations that Gigi had heaped on his head when they'd finally cleared the decks between them. Chief among them was being oblivious to the people who kept his day running as smoothly as it needed to run.

The surprised look he earned from Teresa reinforced Gigi's position.

"You're welcome," the young driver said before quickly climbing behind the wheel of the limo. Not even a Fortune Metals vehicle was allowed to linger in a no-parking zone at the airport.

Swinging the bag over his shoulder, he pulled down the brim of his ball cap and entered the busy terminal. Cora wondered why he wanted to fly commercial sometimes. He'd never told her it was one of the few things that reminded him of simpler times. Like when he'd still been a college student starting up FortuneMedia. When he could walk around freely without being recognized, without bearing the burden of Fortune Metals and all that it entailed.

After going through security, he bought a coffee and with a few minutes to spare, made it to the gate just as his flight was boarding.

The flight attendant welcomed him by name, and he took his seat in first class. Just because he flew commercial now and then didn't mean he'd lost all of his senses.

Twenty minutes later, they were in the air.

He pulled out Walter's last journal, which Teresa had placed in the pocket of his garment bag exactly as Cora had instructed.

He flipped it open to the page marked with the thin black ribbon and began reading from the spot he'd left off last. It wasn't easy. In this last journal, Walter's handwriting had deteriorated considerably. Reeve adjusted the overhead light so he could see better.

Getting old is a blessing and a curse. I read that somewhere. Today it's a curse. My mind remembers clambering around the hillsides as a boy, but my body has forgotten. What else explains tripping over an ottoman that has been in the same spot since Effie put it there? She's been gone for so long, but her sweet smile still haunts me. How can it not when I see it so often on my darling Gigi's face?

Now I have a bandage around my ankle and another reason for my grandson to think I should be put out to pasture. I'm an old man. Junior will get his wish soon enough.

Reeve ruffled the edges of the journal. He was tempted to flip forward pages. Read the ending, as it were. Only the ending of this journal was the ending of Walter Fortune, period.

Reeve did not skip forward.

After complaining about his ankle—evidently it had been sprained and kept Walter off his feet for three weeks—he'd complained about the birds nattering outside his window. Then he'd turned around and sketched surprisingly lifelike pictures of them, only to follow up on the next page with an acidic recounting of the latest Fortune Metals board meeting that he'd attended while sitting in a wheelchair.

Junior insists Dwyer Tusker is a good addition to the board. He's wrong. Tusker's only concerned about himself. But it's the first time Junior's made an independent decision when it comes to the company. I know I need to let him learn from his mistakes. God knows I had to learn from mine. There have been so many.

By the time Reeve arrived at his hotel in Phoenix, he'd read every page.

And he'd only ended up with questions that wouldn't be answered anymore.

At least not by Walter.

He showered off the flight, debated ordering something more substantial than the fruit sitting in a basket alongside several bottles of water, and decided against it. It was already late. He took one of the waters and went out on the balcony that ran around both sides of his corner suite.

The waist-high stone wall was still warm from the heat of the day, but his hair was wet, and the towel wrapped around his hips was damp. He drank down half the bottle of water and set it aside. Cradling his phone in his hand, he studied the names of his family members listed in his contacts.

G. PJ. D for his mother.

Pitifully few.

He'd send Walter's final journal to Gigi, he decided. It was the only one in which their great-grandfather had written about her. And it would mean a lot to her, particularly considering her beloved Grampy had never let her in on the fact that he'd kept a journal at all.

It was also time for her to realize that Walter Fortune was as human as all the rest of them. Just as capable of mistakes and regrets.

Reeve knew she wouldn't want to share the journal later with their father any more than Reeve did.

By the last few entries, Walter hadn't been kind in his assessments of "Junior," stating outright that it had been a mistake to make him CEO of Fortune Metals.

At least no one has died, but I fear he's Edgar and Elias all over again.

Reeve pulled up his most recent text message from his father to finally reply.

If there was a journal, he typed, it's long gone now. He started to hit Send, but hesitated. Sorry, he added, and sent it. He didn't have to wait long for a response.

Doesn't matter anymore.

Reeve shook his head. His father had bugged him constantly for more than a week. Now he didn't care?

Typical PJ.

Reeve finished the bottle of water and went inside the cool room long enough to retrieve another one and then sat on one of the lounges.

The city lights were too bright to allow an impressive starlight display overhead, but there was still something appealing about the desert night air.

Before he could talk himself out of it, he pressed Isabel's name on his phone.

She answered after just two rings. "Is everything all right?" Her voice was filled with sleep.

"I'm in Phoenix. I forgot how late it would be there." Texas was two hours later than Phoenix and the time on his phone had automatically updated.

"You're not, uh, calling to cancel sail—"

"I'm calling because I wanted to hear your voice."

He imagined her expression as she absorbed his admission. Wondered if she'd sucked in her lower lip for a moment. Or if she'd gotten that tiny frown line when she was puzzling out something.

"Oh," she finally said.

It didn't tell him a helluva lot, but the soft way she said it was at least promising.

He smiled and took a long drink of water. His hair and towel had both nearly dried and the heat of the night air was seeping through. "Anything exciting happen today in the world of the *Chatelaine* reporter?"

"As a matter of fact, yes. Not when it comes to the blog, though. Trey's not going to press for me to pay for half the expenses anymore." She sighed softly. Sleepily. "He thought better of it."

More like Trey's father had thought better of it, Reeve thought. But the end result was what counted. *Good work, Cora.* "Congratulations. Now you can close the door on it all."

"I suppose so."

He didn't like the sound of that. "I thought you wanted to."

"I do! But—" She yawned audibly. "I guess I'm still waiting for another shoe to drop. Habit, maybe." She yawned again.

He'd only seen her sleep on an ancient settee. What was her bedroom like? Filled with soft, feminine touches?

He rubbed his closed eyes. "Twenty-one days. Isn't that how long it takes to get over a habit?"

She laughed softly. "I think that's how long it's supposed to take to form a new one."

Heat that had nothing to do with the air temperature was flowing down his spine. He'd already formed a habit where Isabel was concerned, and it hadn't taken anywhere near twenty-one days. "I'll let you get back to counting sheep."

"Wait a second. What're you doing in Phoenix?"

Wanting a woman who needed to get over an old habit. "Got a thing tomorrow with a new branch," he said. "I'll be back tomorrow evening."

"Call me."

It was the most enticing proposition he'd ever received.

"I will," he said. But she'd already hung up.

He exhaled roughly and went back inside the suite.

Another cold shower coming up.

Chapter Thirteen

It's raining.

Isabel looked out her apartment window. The sky was leaden. The street wet. She was so disappointed she could have cried even before Reeve had texted her with his brief weather report.

So much for sailing.

Rain check. No pun intended.

She sent a smiley face.

We'll have to do something else, then...

She waited, staring at her cell phone screen, feeling breathless by the three little dots that told her Reeve was typing something.

How about exploring a Folly? I can pick you up
around ten. Means you get to go back to sleep for
a while.

Her face felt like it might split with her smile. She
was never going to be able to go back to sleep now.

Perfect.

She had enough time to clean her entire apartment
and change her outfit half a dozen times before he
picked her up at her apartment. She finally settled on
deliberately casual cropped pants with a wide-necked,
cropped silk tee. It had been one of her honeymoon
outfits, but there wasn't a single thought of Trey when
she opened her apartment door at Reeve's knock.

When his gaze slid over her as he took her elbow,
she felt like champagne bubbles were rising inside
her.

At the castle, this time Reeve used the main entrance. The security gate was open and unattended.

He parked in the same spot as before and produced a black umbrella that he held over their heads
as they dashed around to the side door. She laughed
when he pulled out the key with as much flourish as
a magician.

"Seems more like trespassing *this* way than getting in by my ordinary means," he admitted when
the lock creaked, and they entered the storage room.

"Can't trespass on what you already own," she reminded lightly. She brushed a few raindrops from her

arms and dashed her fingers through her own hair since she couldn't very well run her fingers through *his.*

"My assistant's looking into the trust."

She couldn't hide her surprise. "Do you think there's something off? Don't you have lawyers and accountants and such to keep it all straight?"

"Entire teams of them," he said. "But I'll still take one Cora over all of them." He shook water from the umbrella and left it upended in the corner of the empty room before leading the way to the old-fashioned kitchen.

Not a single thing had been moved in the two weeks since she'd been there. She felt strangely fond of the old appliances and electric percolator as well as the shrieking hinge of the swinging door. In accord, they made their way to the study where the box of books and photographs was still sitting on the coffee table where he'd left it.

When he pulled the map they'd made from his pocket, she practically bounced on her toes.

To hide it, she went to one of the windows and looked out at the rain. It was falling steadily, and she could see a spout of water coming from a gargoyle. The gush landed on the ground with a splash, causing rivulets in the gravel and dirt.

"Did you check out the Silver Suite when you slept in it?"

She looked over her shoulder at him. "What do you think?"

The corner of his lips lifted, and he made a mark

on the map. "We'll start with the room next to it, then."

"Sounds good to me." She followed him out of the study, and they traipsed through the narrow corridors until, once again, they were standing in the grand foyer with the checkerboard floor. He checked the office for Smitty but the caretaker wasn't there.

They started up the ruby-carpeted staircase and Isabel absently traced the ivy-like engravings on the banister railing. "Did the ceiling in the turret get fixed?"

"According to the bill Cora received." He stopped next to the marble bust on the landing and peered at the face. "I wonder if anyone even knows who that is." Then he shook his head and continued up the stairs.

He was wearing faded blue jeans and a wheat-colored long-sleeved T-shirt with the sleeves pushed up to his elbows. Isabel realized she was watching his rear end and quickly skipped up the stairs until she was even with him.

"He'd be one of you Fortunes," she said. "Wouldn't he? Why have a bust of someone who's entirely anonymous?"

"Why have a castle at all?" he countered wryly. They reached the top of the stairs and he turned toward the bedrooms.

Isabel looked back down the sweeping staircase. At the ornate gold railings of the faux balconies at the base of the stained-glass windows. It was all so beautiful. Yet all so very...lonely.

She shivered slightly and hurried after Reeve. He'd

passed the Silver Suite but she opened the door to glance inside.

Not surprisingly, there was no evidence of it ever having been occupied. No casually thrown blanket over the foot of the massive bed. No opened book on the window seat. She pulled the door closed and joined Reeve at the next bedroom.

"Let me guess," she said, when he moved out of the doorway so she could see. "The Gold Suite?"

He chuckled. "Maybe. Your guess is as good as mine."

They entered the room that was furnished in brilliant gold and deep reds. The bed wasn't as wide as the one in the Silver Suite, but it had an impressive red canopy with half a foot of thick gold fringe hanging down on all sides.

A three-step wooden bench sat next to the bed. "My sister has a dog step so her dog can get up onto the bed. Not as impressive as this human version." She went up onto the first level just so she could peek beneath the red and gold pillow shams at the head of the bed.

The only thing beneath them were silk sheets. No conveniently placed journal.

She carefully arranged the pillows back where they belonged. Reeve was feeling along the shelves inside an ornate gold-leaf armoire.

"I wonder who your great-uncle had in mind when he decorated this place."

"Not Effie." Reeve closed the armoire doors and the tall gold vase on top of it wobbled slightly. He reached up and stilled it. "She didn't like ostentation any more than Walter did."

Isabel looked out the window next to the armoire. She could see the steps leading down from the rear of the castle and the silvery glimmer of water in the distance.

"Maybe it was for Marjorie," he said.

She looked over her shoulder, surprised to hear the name.

"Maybe this whole damn place was for her." He sat on the side of the high bed.

She moved closer, wrapping her hand around the tall gilded bedpost.

"She's the woman who had Wendell's child," he added.

"Rick Maloney," Isabel said before he could continue. "I know the names from..." She trailed off because he already knew it was because of *The Chatelaine Report*.

He blew out a breath and looked at her. "Walter bought her off," he said quietly.

She studied his face. His eyes had turned as cloudy as the sky outside the windows and his jaw looked even tighter than usual. "How do you know?"

He looked down at his palms. "Something he said in his final journal. Walter hadn't approved of Wendell and Marjorie. He thought Wendell was too young and she was too—" He sighed faintly. "*Experienced* was the word he used." He rubbed his temple. "He sent Wendell to Europe and continued providing Marjorie a modest amount of support so long as she dropped any attempts to contact Wendell. If she did, Walter promised her that the money would dry up faster than the Texas plains."

She couldn't help herself. She let go of the bedpost and climbed up to sit next to him. "I'm sorry. Does it help if I tell you that from everything I heard from her grandsons, Marjorie *didn't* strike me as a pillar of innocence?"

"He wrote that he regretted it. But if Walter bought off the woman his brother knocked up, then he was capable of doing it with Luz Cortez, too."

She frowned slightly. "Luz Cortez?"

He picked up her hand, startling her slightly, and lightly rolled her fingers into her palm. "Maribel Sanchez's birth mother. Or so the story goes."

The way he covered her balled fingers with his big palm was distracting. "That was in his final journal, too?"

He shook his head. "Harrison got the info about Luz from Mariana, who got the info from Martin Smith." He swore under his breath and suddenly released her hand.

He didn't need the steps to push off the bed and the bedsprings rocked and creaked softly. "Hearsay." He paced across the room. "But Harrison insists that Mariana is credible."

She watched him pace back again. She wished there were something she could do to take the lines of strain from his face. "Reeve, just talk to Mariana yourself. How can that be any worse than—"

she waved her hand at him "—all this uncertainty you're feeling?"

"I'm not uncertain."

He was exasperating. "Then why are you so bothered?"

"What I'm *bothered* by is you."

She yanked her head back at the sudden change of direction. "Don't worry," she said stiffly. "I have no interest in writing—" She sucked in her words when he planted his hands on either side of her hips.

The mattress squeaked again as he leaned close. "You know this isn't about *The Chatelaine Report.*"

Every nerve ending in her entire body went on alert. She felt suddenly tense and weak all at the same time. It was alarming and delicious, and she almost wished that he would just put his hands on her so she wouldn't have to think any more about why it was too soon. Why she needed some time and some space before she fell headlong into another relationship.

Particularly with Reeve Fortune, who didn't do relationships at all.

But making him responsible for solving her attraction to him was an absolute coward's way out.

She tipped her head until her forehead rested on his chest. She could feel the steady, deep thump of his heart. It was much, much steadier than her own.

Then his hand gently cupped the back of her neck. She lifted her head. His eyes searched hers.

"If I kiss you, I'm not going to want to stop," he murmured.

She inhaled shakily. "Me either."

The clouds had gone from his eyes to be replaced by a flicker of blue flame. "Then we should probably get off the bed."

She dropped her gaze to the quick quirk on his lips. Why hadn't she noticed before how perfectly shaped they were? How full and mobile and capable of expression? "Probably," she agreed faintly.

Only neither one of them made a move to vacate the bed.

Instead, he grazed his fingers down her cheek. Her throat. Along her bare shoulder, stopping only when he reached the silk of her T-shirt.

She could hardly breathe. Her nipples tightened and that delicious tension coiled deep inside her until she felt like she was vibrating from it.

Then his gaze flickered. His teeth bared slightly as he yanked out his phone to glare at it.

She realized it had been silently ringing.

He turned away, lifting it to his ear. *"What?"* he practically growled.

She sagged, pressing her hand to her chest, willing her heart to stop racing.

"No." His voice turned flat. "I do not want to talk to him. I've made my position clear. So far, I'm not actively working against him." He walked out of the room. "Tell your client to be grateful and say thank you."

She slid off the bed and walked over to the window again. Her knees felt wobbly. It was a strange sensation. One she hadn't felt before. Not with Trey. Not with anyone.

She distracted herself by focusing on the statue nearest to the castle.

Was it a tribute to Effie? The sister-in-law who'd been more of a mother to Wendell than his own?

Or to Marjorie? The woman who had—by design or by accident—borne him a son. Had he come back home from his travels older, wiser, but still loving her? Had she refused him and *that's* why he left again after building this crazy castle?

No matter which way Isabel looked at it, it seemed extraordinarily sad. Instead of living out his life where his brother lived, where his *son* had lived, Wendell had gone away and never returned.

She chewed the inside of her cheek and glanced at Reeve. He was pacing across the landing strip of a hallway with his phone still pressed to his ear.

She went back to the bed and tugged on the velvet bedspread until it looked straight and smooth and once more, untouched. When she was done, Reeve had finished his phone call and was standing in the doorway of the room.

She walked toward him. "Everything okay?"

"As okay as it can be right now." His hands closed over her hips and he pulled her up against him.

She sucked in air, cupping her hands instinctively around his arms. Everything about him was hard. Except the look in his eyes and the inviting perfection of his mouth. "I, uh, I thought we weren't—"

"We won't." His head lowered toward hers. "Trust me."

Desire was flooding her, but the words still made

her laugh. "My mama told me to *never* believe a man who says *trust me*. Particularly when he's got a certain look in his eyes."

His lips curved. "Then we'll have to trust you," he murmured, and kissed her.

And it was…glorious.

She could no more resist than she could stop the rain from falling.

She was vaguely aware of him lifting her right off her feet and she curled her arms tightly around his shoulders. Her fingers slid through his thick, surprisingly silky hair. His tongue teased hers and his fingers splayed against the bare skin of her back beneath her shirt, then ran down her rear, lifting her thighs.

She linked her ankles behind him and pulled her mouth from his to haul in an urgent breath.

Everything about him was right.

The way he smelled. Tasted.

The way he felt. The way he felt her.

"Waiting is overrated," she breathed, arching against him in search of relief, even if it was only the feel of his heart thudding against hers.

"I usually think so." He bowed his head, pressing his forehead against her shoulder. His hand slid up her ribs.

She groaned and pulled his hand until it covered her breast. And groaned even more when his fingers slid aside the thin fabric of her bra to reach her bare, tight nipple. She worked her head around, tugging his hair. "Kiss me. Kiss me and kiss me—"

He did. And he did. And he did.

He carried her back inside the gold room, pressing her flat against the closed front of the armoire. The vase on top wobbled and fell off, landing harmlessly on the bed next to it.

"Ahem!"

Reeve's head jerked back and over his shoulder, Isabel could see Smitty standing in the doorway. Instead of a crowbar, this time he was holding a bucket and a mop.

And judging by his expression, she suspected he'd been "ahemming" more than once.

Feeling flushed, she unlinked her ankles and slowly slid her feet down to the floor, thankful for Reeve's solid body blocking her as she hastily adjusted her bra and pulled her shirt back where it belonged.

As for Reeve, he just continued looking over his shoulder at the man. "How're you doing, Smitty?"

"Not as good as you," the man said drily. He lifted his mop. "Got a leak in the great hall." With his bucket clanking, he turned and left.

But the damage—or reprieve, depending on her wavering viewpoint—was done.

She bit her upper lip and retied the fabric belt of her linen pants, looking anywhere other than Reeve. "Saved by the rain."

"Cursed by it," he countered.

She pressed her lips together, unexpectedly wanting to smile.

But then he did, shaking his head slightly as he blew out a rueful laugh.

Letting her own smile loose, she rolled the vase closer so she could grab hold of it properly. "Here." She started to hand it to him but stopped when her fingers brushed something inside the mouth of it.

She stuck her fingers down deeper and worked out the object.

They both stared at it.

Then Reeve slowly reached for the journal that had been rolled into a tube. The rubber bands fastened around it were dried out and shrunken and quickly fell apart, leaving just one that clung valiantly to the leather until Reeve uncurled the journal. Then it, too, gave up the ghost and fell away.

He looped his arm over her shoulder, and she held one side of the book while he held the other. The curl in it was strong. Probably set in by decades.

Isabel traced the embossed monogram and numbers on the cover with her fingertip. "Nineteen seventy-six."

"That's the year my grandfather died. Philip Sr."

She pressed her cheek against his arm. "And this makes sixteen journals now?"

"Yes."

She looked up at him. "You want to sit down and start reading right this minute?"

"After learning about him paying off Marjorie?" His lips twisted. "I don't think I want to read it at all."

She ran her hand up and down his spine. "One act doesn't have to contradict everything else that you know about him."

"I hope you're right." He let the journal spring

back into its adopted tube shape and left it lying on the bed. "Suppose we should see how bad this leak is." He placed the vase back on top of the armoire and wrapped his free hand around hers. "It's long past time that we got a maintenance company to take care of this place."

She tugged on her hand. "You're not going to fire an old man!"

He raised his brows. "Did I say that?"

"Well, no, but—"

"Smitty doesn't need to be going around with mops and crowbars at his age." He lifted her hand and kissed her knuckles, his vivid blue eyes watching her from beneath his thick lashes. "Doesn't mean he can't order around the ones who do."

Her smile felt shaky. Not because she didn't believe him.

But because she did.

They left the room and followed the echoing sounds of clanking metal down to the grand foyer.

Smitty was already inside the great hall, mopping up a large puddle of water near one of the tall mullioned windows. He'd thrown down a stack of rags nearby.

He was moving slowly but steadily, but even from across the huge space, they could hear him huffing and puffing.

"I'll find a chair for him," Reeve said quietly.

She nodded and hurried across the floor, her espadrilles squeaking against the marble. "Here," she reached for the mop handle. "Let me do that, Smitty."

"I got it," he said irritably.

"I know you do. But you said this place had never had a woman's touch." She grinned at him. "So here's your chance."

He chuckled and released the mop. "I did say that, miss. And I meant it, too." He waved a gnarled hand. "This room's meant for ladies in fine gowns and men falling over themselves to get their attention. Yet I don't think it's ever hosted so much as a square dance."

She smiled as she wrung out the thick ropy strands of the cotton mop. "I've been to plenty of square dances." Mostly her father's attempt to counteract the much more traditional cotillion classes that her mother had insisted on. "None of them were on marble floors with Gothic arches overhead. A fancy-dress ball, though? That seems totally in keeping."

"Or a wedding," Smitty said.

She gave him a quick look, not sure he wasn't making some reference to her wedding-that-wasn't. But his expression looked perfectly innocent.

She slopped the mop back into the pool of water. "Are you troubled with a lot of leaks around the castle?"

"A few. Windows in here have always been a problem." He bent over and spread out a few of the rags that he began pushing around with his thick-soled shoe. "Least since I've been around."

Reeve joined them, carrying one of the benches from the foyer on his shoulder as if he were used to lugging heavy antiques around.

He placed it well away from the water's reach. "Sit down, Smitty."

"I don't—" The old man's lips compressed when Reeve gave him a look.

"Getting old sucks," he muttered, but he gave up pushing around his rags and sat down. He pulled a handkerchief from his pocket and wiped his sweaty forehead.

"It's better than the alternative," Reeve countered. "My grandfather died when he was only forty. Think everyone would've much preferred for him to get old."

Smitty made a sound. He folded his arms across his dull blue work shirt. "That was a sad day," he agreed.

Isabel handed Reeve the mop while she carried several rags over to the window. She could see a trail of water working its way from the lower right corner and she rolled up one of the rags and wedged it into the sill. It wouldn't stop the rain from coming in, but it would at least slow it down. "I meant to ask you last time, Smitty. How long have you worked here at the castle?"

"Oh, a long time, miss. Long, long time."

"You'd have to, if you knew my grandfather," Reeve said. "For some reason, I was thinking you'd started here under PJ's watch." He wrung out the mop with enough deftness that Isabel couldn't hide her surprise.

"What?" He spread his hands. "I can mop."

She met Smitty's eyes. He looked amused, too.

"Clearly," she told Reeve mildly.

He shook his head. "I own a damn boat," he muttered under his breath as he applied the mop once more to the small flood. "Gotta clean it, too."

"PJ is—"

"Philip Jr.," Isabel provided Smitty. She toed off her espadrilles and tossed them off to one side so they wouldn't get even wetter. "Reeve's father."

"Ah, right. Sure." Smitty was nodding. "He married that French girl."

"Delphine," Reeve said. "Isn't there a wet vac around here? This would go a lot faster if we could just suck up the water."

Smitty shook his head. "No sir. Got a sump pump for the cellar in the shed. Sometimes the pond gets too big for its britches but haven't had to run it in years."

"Didn't know the shed had a cellar."

"Nothing down there these days except old jars and leftover tiles."

"Well." Reeve propped his arm atop the mop handle. "Get on the phone and order a vac from whoever can deliver it the quickest. And while you're at it, see if there are any glaziers in the area. This window probably isn't the only one that needs tending. If you can't find someone local, let me know. I have a facilities director at Fortune Metals who can handle it."

"If you think I'm not taking proper care—"

Reeve lifted his hand peaceably. "Not saying anything of the sort, Smitty."

"Better not be," the old man grumbled. He grunted as he pushed to his feet and walked slowly out of the room.

Isabel leaned close to Reeve. "And you think you're going to be able to soothe his ruffled ego when you hire a maintenance company?"

"Maybe I'll let you tell him."

"Chicken."

The corners of his eyes crinkled. "Yes, miss—" he did a dead-on imitation of Smitty "—you got that right."

She laughed softly and added another towel to the little dam that she'd created.

It took nearly an hour for them to get the water mopped up. Isabel was on her hands and knees drying the floor with the last of the rags while Reeve dumped out the bucket of water for the third time when Frank Sinatra music suddenly filled the room.

She sat back on her knees, smiling at Smitty as he entered the great hall. His smug expression was enough to tell her he was responsible.

"That's what I'm talking about, miss," he said, and held out his hand to her.

Delighted, she tossed aside her rag, stood and did a quick curtsy before taking his hand and he turned her into a slow, but very capable, waltz.

They'd nearly circled the entire space when Reeve returned.

He waited until they passed him and then he tapped Smitty's shoulder. "May I cut in?"

The caretaker formally transferred her hand to Reeve. "I wondered if I was going to have to send you my dancing director for you to get the hint."

"Figured I'd give you a few minutes to remember

how it feels to hold a pretty girl's hand," Reeve countered. He placed his hand lightly on Isabel's back.

"Now that's not something I'm ever likely to forget." Smitty's laugh sounded rusty as he headed over to sit on the bench again. "Old or not."

Reeve looked at Isabel. His thumb gently stroked her hand. "Remember your cotillion classes?"

She felt too oddly choked to speak. So she just nodded and placed her hand on his shoulder.

He winked imperceptibly and swung her into a smooth waltz. And when "Moon River" melded into "Cheek to Cheek," he twirled her perfectly around into a foxtrot that made her throw back her head and laugh breathlessly.

The murals overhead spun and so did Reeve and Isabel.

Dance after dance after dance.

And whether it was too soon or not, Isabel knew that she was dangerously close to falling head over heels for Reeve.

Chapter Fourteen

"You *danced*?" Paige sighed wistfully as she dried a plate and handed it to Ronnie who handed it to Isabel who placed it in the cupboard. "I wish I could get Ted to dance. Really dance, you know? Not just shuffle around with his hands on my hips."

It was Sunday evening, and they were at their parents' house for dinner. And just like old times, the girls had to do the dishes. Not like old times, they'd spent an hour before dinner repackaging wedding gifts to be returned to sender along with a personalized note that Isabel had handwritten. Thirty-two of them.

Because—as she'd told Trey when he'd turned up his nose at some of the gifts—not everyone *liked* sending money as a gift.

"That shuffling around with his hands on my hips

is how Blake and I ended up with Sasha," Ronnie was saying drily.

Paige ignored her. "It's *so* romantic."

"What's romantic?" Auntie Pearl strode into the room in search of her after-dinner brandy.

"Reeve Fortune dancing with Issa," Ronnie provided.

Since nobody else in the family could stand brandy, Isabel's mom routinely hid it away in a cupboard. Isabel pulled it out and handed it to her aunt along with the snifter that was only ever used by Pearl. It had an ornate pattern of gold around the rim that reminded Isabel of the castle.

As if she needed any reminding.

Pearl uncapped the bottle and filled the glass at least two times fuller than etiquette decreed. "Reeve Fortune. He's the one who wants to sue you, isn't he?"

"Old news, Auntie." Another plate passed between the sisters.

"Those Fortunes are a different breed," Pearl said. "Kidnappings and all manner of craziness."

"That was ages ago," Isabel said. "And an entirely different branch of the family." She knew, because at her old company, she'd covered the scandalous story of tech billionaire Gerald Robinson turning out to be a supposedly dead Jerome Fortune and the fallout that had occurred when he left an unstable wife to marry his longtime love.

"Still. Blood tells. And their blood is not like ours." Pearl lifted her snifter and wrinkled her nose as she drank.

"For heaven's sake! The Fortunes aren't from another planet. They're wealthy." Isabel closed the cupboard on the last plate with a snap. "It doesn't excuse
them from happiness or grief. Reeve pulls his pants
on one leg at a time just like everyone else."

"Tut tut tut." Pearl raised her eyebrows. "And do
you know that from personal experience, missy?"

Isabel's face got hot. "I'm thirty-two years old,
Auntie. My personal experiences are my business.
But as it happens, nothing like that is going on." *Only
because you were interrupted by a not-so-shy castle
caretaker.*

"Nothing like *what* is going on?" Lydia entered
the kitchen, carrying the remainder of the angel food
cake they'd had for dessert.

"Issa hasn't had sex yet with Reeve Fortune," Ronnie told their mother with a wicked grin.

"My sex life is not up for discussion!"

"Thank God for that," her father said, entering the
kitchen just in time to hear her, and leaving again
just as quickly.

Isabel dropped her dish towel over her head and
groaned.

"I've always thought sex was overrated," Pearl
said.

"That's because you've never been in love," Lydia
pointed out acerbically. "Sex with the man you love
is—" She kissed her fingertips and smiled.

Pearl grimaced and left the room.

Lydia winked at her daughters and followed.

Isabel sat down at the kitchen table. "Sunday dinners did not used to involve talk like this."

"Sunday dinners used to be dull as dirt," Ronnie said. "Plus," she said as she swatted Paige on the shoulder with her dish towel, "we can talk about sex now that baby-Paigey's beyond the age of consent." She looked out the window that overlooked the fenced backyard to check on Sasha and Penny who were playing outside now that the weekend-long rain had finally ended. Then she sat down across from Isabel. "So. What's really going on with you and Reeve?"

She willed her face not to flush. Considering she was the lone brunette among her sisters, it seemed entirely unfair that she was also the only one with the tendency to blush. "Nothing's going on."

Paige pulled out a chair and sat, too. "He's not the reason you called it off with Trey?"

Isabel's jaw loosened. "I hardly even *knew* him before I called it off with Trey."

"Not according to Trey's mama," Paige said. She leaned her chair back, balancing it on the two rear legs the way she'd always done. "I heard it from a friend who heard it from a friend that she's been telling her society biddies that Trey had a narrow escape since you were already involved elsewhere."

Isabel's jaw tightened.

"None of them would be getting away with saying anything if that picture of Trey and his naked squeeze hadn't disappeared," Ronnie said. "If anyone had a narrow escape, it's you. But that doesn't mean

I believe that nothing's going on with Reeve now. I mean you danced in a castle!" She spread her hands.

Isabel didn't need to close her eyes to remember the sheer delight she'd felt. A delight that even now made her feel weak in her knees and shaky in her heart. "A dance doesn't equal love." If she said it often enough, maybe she'd convince herself. "What kind of person would I be if I went from nearly marrying someone—sleazeball or not—to falling for someone else practically before the sun sets?"

Ronnie smiled slightly, but there was no missing the concern in her eyes. "I think it just makes you human, Issa. Like all the rest of us, it makes you human."

When Isabel drove home later that evening, she found herself driving past the Third Community Church.

The parking lot was crammed full of cars. A limousine sat nearby.

Another wedding, no doubt. It was the season for them.

She kept driving. The Fortune Metals tower was visible on the horizon, and she wondered if Reeve was there. Working.

As much as she'd hoped she'd see him that day, after he'd driven her back to her apartment the day before, he hadn't said a single thing about when he'd see her next.

She'd told herself that was a good thing. Pumping

the brakes on what felt like a runaway train *had* to be a good thing. Didn't it?

It made absolutely no sense, then, when she turned in the direction of the tower. There was little traffic this late on a Sunday evening, and she quickly reached the empty parking lot surrounding the massive complex.

She parked under a tree, rolled down her window and turned off the engine as she studied the buildings in the twilight. A shopping mall was on one side of the high-rise. A grassy park was on the other.

She followed the line of windows up the building. Some were illuminated. More of them were not. Near the top of the building, they were all ablaze.

When her phone buzzed beside her, she jumped guiltily, as if she'd been caught doing something she shouldn't.

It was just her mom calling to remind her to drop off the repackaged gifts at the post office.

"I won't forget, Mom." How could she when they completely filled her back seat? "Soon as the post office opens tomorrow."

"Good girl. Drive carefully. I love you."

"Love you, too."

She dropped the phone on her passenger seat next to another wobbly stack of packages and folded her arms atop the steering wheel as she eyed Reeve's building once more. In her mind, though, she was in his arms, skipping across the marble floor of the great hall. When her phone buzzed again a moment later, she grabbed it again. "I won't forget the ones you put in my trunk, either," she said.

"Glad to hear it," Reeve answered.

The phone slid right out of her hand, and she swept the floor between her legs for it. "Sorry," she said breathlessly, when she found it once more and hit the speaker button. "Dropped the phone for a sec. What's, uh, what's up*?" Excellent, Issa. Great way to sound breezy.*

"Are you busy tomorrow?"

"Besides a trip to the post office?" She pressed her palm to her chest where her heart felt like it was skittering around on a hot griddle. "Not...not really."

"I'm going to Rambling Rose."

She barely had time to inhale the surprise of that when he continued.

"Interested in going?"

"Sure." It came out more like a croak. She cleared her throat and tried again. "What time?" As if that mattered.

"Early. I have a meeting I need to get back for in Chatelaine."

Right. Because he didn't take time off work for anyone. "Would it help if I met you?"

"No. I'll pick you up at seven."

"Okay," she said, but he'd already disconnected.

She blinked a little at the abruptness, then called Ronnie and told her about it. "What do I do?"

"Set your alarm clock for one thing," Ronnie said drily. "And be ready when he comes to get you."

"But he didn't exactly sound enthusiastic."

"Issa," her sister chided. "He could have gone to Rambling Rose without you. What do you want? Mariachis? You had that already, remember?"

Isabel pressed her fingertips to her forehead. "You're right. Of course, you're right."

"Call me afterward. I'm dying to know how it turns out."

"For Mariana?"

Ronnie laughed. "Yeah. Sure. For her, too." Then she hung up.

Isabel blew out a breath and lifted her head. She started the car again, turned on her headlights and trolled closer to the building, braking when she was level with the main entrance. The lobby was lit and empty except for a lone man sitting behind a long reception desk. As she watched, he clearly noticed her car. He stood and walked toward the doors.

Security guard, she suspected. He wore a white shirt and dark pants. When he lifted a walkie-talkie and spoke into it, she was certain.

The last thing she wanted was to be caught loitering outside Reeve's building.

She hastily took her foot off the brake and because of her stacks of boxes, circumspectly turned in a big loop that took her back to the entrance. By the time she turned out of the parking lot, a security vehicle had arrived and was idling in front of the building where she'd been.

Twenty-five floors above, Reeve watched a nondescript car meander around the empty parking lot below while Gigi's voice came through his speaker phone. "I really enjoyed today, Reeve," she was saying. "It's been so long since we golfed."

"No," he corrected. "It's been a long time since *I* golfed, which is why you whipped my butt."

She laughed lightly. "Brother, I always beat you on the green and you know it."

It was true. He'd had the long game. She'd had the short.

He looked down at the photograph that Cora had given him. "Do you remember when Walter bought the Stellar building in Chatelaine?"

"No, but I remember he'd had plans for it," she said, "A bed-and-breakfast or something like that. He just didn't find the time to make it happen. That's why I was so angry when I thought you intended to tear down the building."

"He never told you anything else about it?" He turned away from the windows and returned to his desk and the concise report that Cora had prepared for him.

"Not that I can think of. Why?"

"Pedro and Antonia Cortez," he said instead of answering. "He was a pharmacist at the drugstore in Chatelaine," he added into the silence that followed.

"Luz's parents, I assume," she finally said.

"Luz and her sister, Alma. According to Cora, they were twins. Pedro had a good job. A home. Yet the family moved away in 1935. One day there. The next day gone."

"How old were Luz and Alma?"

"Twenty." He squared the grainy black-and-white photograph of a two-story house with a pitched roof. Cora's report had been typically detailed. "And guess where they'd lived."

She waited a beat. *"No."* She drew out the word. "The *Stellar* building?"

"None other." He leaned back in his chair and rubbed his hand down his face. "Walter bought three whole blocks in Chatelaine just so he could get hold of the house where Luz had once lived. No one would have reason to suspect it was the house that had been his real interest." He exhaled and sat forward again. "Did you know that Walter and Effie's marriage had been arranged?"

"Don't be ridiculous."

His jaw tightened slightly. But he reminded himself that Gigi didn't have all the information that he did, and he was part of the reason for that, since he'd willfully kept Walter's journals to himself. "Look. I know it's late, but can we just meet to talk about this? Are you in town?"

"Yes. Harrison's here."

"Sit tight. I'm on my way." He ended the call and shoved Cora's report, the photograph and the records she'd compiled from the Fortune Trust into his briefcase. He took the elevator down to the lobby.

The security guard on duty immediately hopped out of his chair, discreetly wiping a few crumbs from his tie. "Done for the night, Mr. Fortune?"

"I am, George." Thank God for name badges. The security guards changed so often that Reeve had given up trying to match the names to the right faces. "Quiet night so far?"

"It's always quiet at night here, sir."

"That's what we want," Reeve assured him, and headed for the private entrance around the back of the lobby.

It didn't take long to drive to Gigi's place. She lived in the same gated community where he'd lived before moving out to Aransas Pass. She was waiting with the door open and a longneck bottle of Rising Fortune IPA for him in her hand.

She'd changed out of her golf togs into a floaty kind of dress that made her seem softer than usual. More of the Harrison effect, he thought, greeting the other man as he followed her into the house.

They sat down in her living room. Gigi and Harrison on the couch. Reeve facing them. For once, it didn't strike him as him versus them.

They were all in this together.

He took the items from his briefcase and spread them on the coffee table between them. The photo. Cora's reports. And Walter's last journal. Embossed with the year he died right below his initials.

Her gaze latched onto it greedily and he twisted open his beer, took a long drink and then set it aside. He was surprised that she didn't pick up the journal. As if she were wary of what it contained.

His sister always had been the smart one.

"Walter and Effie," he said. "It was an arranged marriage, whether you want to hear it or not, Gigi."

"He loved her. I know he did. He talked about her all the time, Reeve."

"You're right. He did love her." He waved his hand at the leather-bound journal. "He frequently wrote about that. But it didn't start out that way. I'd suspected it from what he wrote in other journals, but I'm convinced of it now." Since she still hadn't reached for the book, he picked it up and flipped it open to the page he'd marked with the thin black ribbon. Even though he'd gone over it so many times now he had nearly memorized it, his throat still felt tight when he read it aloud.

"'Will she greet me with welcome in her heart? Or when my day comes, will my sins send me to another place altogether?'"

He looked at Gigi and silently handed the book to her. Her brow knit as she took it. Reeve noticed the way she reached for Harrison's hand. And the way that Harrison took it in his.

Like Reeve, she read aloud.

"'She was my beloved wife. But in my deepest recesses, I've still harbored memories of that youthful love that couldn't be. Was that my punishment, then? To fall in love with the woman I married, even though she wasn't the one I'd have chosen? Is that why I lost her as well? So long ago now, that I hardly remember how cornered I'd felt by my father's demands. And poor, dear Effie with even fewer choices. Life wasn't fair to women then. It's often not fair, now. I never had the heart—'"

Gigi's voice faltered. She sniffed and moistened her lips and forged on.

"'—to tell Gigi that. *My sweet Gigi, who's the image of her great-grandmother.*'"

Harrison handed her a handkerchief, and she swiped her eyes. "His handwriting is so bad," she said huskily. "It's practically illegible in some spots."

"He'd had a stroke," Reeve said. "It's a wonder he wrote anything at all."

"I know. I know." She exhaled shakily and began again. Her eyes were still wet.

"'*I know she didn't have it easy, but she stood by me. If I'd been a better man, would God have spared us all? Would we have still lost Philip? It broke her. It broke me, too. As much as it broke me when I lost her, such a short time after that.*'"

"'*No amount of riches can fill the hole in my soul.*'"

Her voice broke on that last. She wiped her nose again. "The youthful love. You think he's referring to Luz? And he bought her family home practically a lifetime later, just because he'd never forgotten her."

He nodded. "Until Cora told me about the house, I hadn't paid much attention to that 'memory' bit. I'd even thought there was a possibility that he might have paid off Luz the way he'd paid off Marjorie Maloney."

"*What?*"

He backed up and filled her in.

"I can't believe it," she said. "Paying off someone—" She pressed her lips together for a moment.

"I was going to say it's something we don't do, but—" She exhaled and reached for Harrison's hand again.

"Let's focus on the Luz issue," Harrison prompted. "One thing at a time."

"He's right." Reeve tapped the photograph of the Cortez/Stellar house. "Once I learned about the house, it all fell together. We'll never know if their affair happened before or after Walter married Effie in 1935. But the Cortez family moved away from Chatelaine that same year. Lock, stock and barrel. No records of where they went after that. And you know Cora."

"If there was more information to find, she'd have found it," Gigi said.

"Exactly." He looped his fingers together. "Say Luz was pregnant. By a newly married man, or by one who was soon to be married, whether he wanted to be or not. Either way, what kind of prospects did *she* have?"

"So the family moves away," Harrison finally spoke. "Baby Maribel is placed at the foundling hospital after she's born, and the rest is history."

"And Grampy never did know."

Reeve nodded. "He never knew. But now *we* do." He picked up his beer bottle. "Which means we have to see Mariana Sanchez."

Gigi's fingers trembled as she brushed back her hair. "If only I hadn't dismissed her so easily, I—"

"We both did," he cut her off. "But that's not all there is."

She lifted her palm. "What else is there?"

"The Fortune Trust," he said.

"What about it?"

"You know the trust holds a myriad of oddball assets. Property. Jewelry." He nodded toward the ruby-and-diamond ring on Gigi's finger that had once been Effie's. "Accounts going back even further than Walter's parents. The list goes on and on. I asked Cora to give me an accounting, because I was afraid that PJ was up to something. She didn't find his fingerprints specifically on any transactions. But she did realize that something was missing. An old venture that Walter and Wendell operated outside of the Fortune Mining Company."

"I don't understand. Why would they do that?"

Reeve spread his hands. "I don't know. But Cora knew about it. She'd notarized some paperwork for them once when she first started working for Walter that ensured the drilling company would stay under the trust if anything ever happened to one or the other of them. Maybe they were being extra cautious after the mine collapse in '65. Who knows? Only now, she can't find any record of it."

"Drilling companies come and go," Gigi said. "Maybe it petered out."

"Maybe. But at the time, it was profitable as hell." He looked at Gigi. "More profitable than Fortune Mining, if what Cora says is true."

Gigi laughed, shaking her head. "That's not possible."

"A lot of things that we didn't think possible are turning out to be very possible."

"So where was this drilling company based? If it wasn't part of Fortune Mining—"

"Southwestern part of the state." Reeve felt his jaw tighten again. "The name of the venture was Cortezalita Drilling. And what made it so profitable was the fact that they'd found gold. Lots of gold. And now... Poof." He flicked his fingers in the air. "It's magically disappeared from the Fortune Trust. Cora thinks it happened during PJ's reign." He grimaced.

"Grampy never wrote about the gold in his journals?"

"Not the ones I've seen. But if Walter continually kept one throughout his life, there are a lot of years unaccounted for. And who knows what they might contain."

Chapter Fifteen

Isabel set two different alarm clocks to ensure that she didn't oversleep the next morning.

As a result, she was fully awake, dressed in another one of her non-honeymoon outfits and watching for Reeve's car, when it pulled up in front of her apartment.

Fortunately, a strong cup of coffee hid the fact that excitement had kept her awake nearly all night and she skipped out to his car even before he had a chance to get out.

"Good morning." His eyes were bluer than the sky as he reached across to push open the door from the inside. "You look pretty."

She grinned, feeling much too giddy for this early in the day. "So do you. Look good, I mean."

His lips twitched, she pulled the door closed and fastened her seat belt, and they were off. He handed her one of the to-go cups that were sitting in his console. "I'd have brought bacon but figured coffee would do."

She smiled. "It's a tolerable substitute."

His smile widened slightly. "Gigi and Harrison are going to meet us in Rambling Rose. At that market-place where Mariana's food truck is located."

"Oh!" She didn't know why she felt so surprised. It was only natural that Reeve would have his sister along when meeting Mariana for the first time.

"You know her, right?"

"Gigi?" Barely. "Just because of her podcast." Which Gigi recorded at Stellar Productions.

"Harrison Vasquez is one of our lawyers. And her fiancé." His gaze slid over her. "He wasn't the one who sent you the threatening letter."

"Well, that's something," she said with feeling.

He drove down the block and when they passed the museum, she thought again about the visit she'd made there. Just two weeks ago, but it felt longer.

"How was dinner with your folks yesterday?"

"Fine." She took a drink of the coffee—it was strong but laced with a heavy dose of delicious cream—and set it back in the cup holder. "We packed up all the wedding gifts that need to be sent back. I just need to drop them off at the post office and mail them all." She dusted her hands together. "And that is the end of that. What about you? How was your day?" What had sparked his about-face when it came to meeting Mariana?

"I went golfing with Gigi."

"Sounds fun."

"If you call it fun to have your sister beat you by five strokes."

She smiled. "What a bruise to the ego."

"Then I went to the office."

"On a Sunday?" She looked out the side window. There was no way that she was going to admit to her brief stalking of his office building.

"Cora had prepared some stuff for me. It's what prompted this trip."

Isabel angled in her seat so she could watch him. His profile was sharp and clear against the morning light. "Want to talk about it or should I just sit here and continue speculating?"

"Walter definitely had an affair with Luz."

She held back her "I told you so" but only because his expression looked so solemn.

"You know about him buying those blocks of property in Chatelaine. What I didn't know until yesterday evening was that one of the buildings—Stellar's, in fact—used to be the home of Luz Cortez and her family."

She stared. "Seriously?"

"He bought it when Gigi and I were kids. He didn't turn it into any sort of business, though Gigi said he talked about it. He bought it and held on to it out of pure sentimentality for a girl he'd once loved. Luz. And I think you were right. That he never knew there'd been a baby."

She'd never felt less like crowing over being right.

"What do you plan to do about it? Besides meeting Mariana, I mean."

His thumb drummed the steering wheel. "Harrison will come prepared. She's a legal heir. A grandchild. Comes before the great-grandchildren."

Isabel hadn't even thought about that. "I still don't think she's interested in the financial aspect of it. She wants to meet her family members. Simple as that. Does she know you're coming?"

"Yes. And once she meets us, she might decide it's not that much of an appealing prospect after all."

She leaned toward him. "I think you're *very* wrong about that."

He gave her a sidelong glance. "We'll see."

Her heart skittered around. Not because of his words. But because of the hand he slid oh-so-briefly behind her neck.

And it kept skittering all the rest of the way to Rambling Rose.

Gigi's fiancé turned out to be a tall, handsome man with black hair and eyes as dark a brown as Isabel's. He shook her hand warmly when Reeve introduced them after they parked next to each other at Mariana's Market.

As for Gigi, she looked as picture-perfect as she always did, her thick blond hair waving over the shoulders of the ivory blouse she'd paired with equally ivory palazzo pants. "Love the sundress," she told Isabel. "I can never wear that shade of peach. Washes me right out." She was talking quickly, almost as if she were nervous, which seemed hard to believe. "I brought this." She held up a small picture album. "Do you think I should bring it or—"

Harrison dropped his arm around her shoulders. "Bring it."

"Now that we've got the chitchat out of the way, let's get this done."

Gigi met Isabel's eyes. "My brother. Once he's ready to move, he's ready."

"And you're any different?" Reeve wrapped his fingers around Isabel's elbow and she shivered a little despite the sun that was already warm in the sky. As one, their quartet turned and approached the haphazardly arranged vendors who'd set up shop. There were tents and trailers and a myriad of sellers.

"I told you it was quite the place," Harrison said. He was the only one who'd been there before, and he capably led the way through an array of homemade crafts, foods, and even furniture to a central aisle dominated by the large shining food truck positioned at one end.

"Mariana's" was painted across the outside of it in scrolling letters. Green-and-white market umbrellas made an even more picturesque display, shading the picnic tables arranged in one long row leading up to the truck.

Two of the tables were occupied by a half dozen people who were clearly watching their approach with suspicion.

Isabel was surprised when she recognized Lincoln Fortune Maloney among them. Though when she thought about it, she shouldn't have been. Since learning they were Wendell's heirs, Linc and his siblings were all part of the same strange case of Wendell and Walter Fortune.

Mariana was the only older woman in the group, and as such would have been easy to pick out even without the protective stance the others seemed to have toward her.

"I wasn't expecting a convention," Reeve said under his breath. He was also surprised. Isabel figured it was the reason why he squeezed her hand so tightly in his.

"It'll be fine. I know Linc and his siblings." To prove it, she lifted her free hand in a deliberately friendly wave to Max, Cooper, Damon and Justine as they approached the tables and greeted them by name. It was enough to break the ice, and between her and Harrison, introductions were soon out of the way.

Meanwhile, Gigi had approached Mariana, who'd also stood.

Despite the age difference, Isabel immediately saw the resemblance between the two women. It was there in the shape of their eyes. The line of their jaw.

"I'm sorry," she heard Gigi whisper as she offered her slender hand to the buxom older woman with a big blond bun on top of her head. "I'm so sorry for not believing you earlier."

"Ah, now, honey." Mariana had a wide smile on her face that was a little tremulous around the corners. "You don't know me, so you don't know I don't do handshakes. 'Specially with my own kin, whether we know each other or not." She just reached out and tugged Gigi close, giving her a big hug.

Despite Gigi's obvious shock, she got over it quickly, and with a choked laugh, she hugged the woman right back.

"You too, handsome," Mariana said, beckoning Reeve closer with her hand. "You don't get off the hook, either."

Isabel's eyes dampened at the vaguely hunted look that he sent her. She knew the kind of upbringing he'd had. The lack of affection from his own parents. Now here was Mariana—a complete stranger except for the genetics that connected them—accepting him so naturally, even despite the months of his resistance. She gave him a little push, and looking entirely un-Reeve-like, he went and submitted to Mariana's hug.

As if she knew exactly how he felt, the woman held on long enough to get over even his disquiet, and when she finally let him go, Isabel had to bite back a smile at the dusky red that filled his cheeks.

"Come on now," Mariana invited everyone to sit back down around the tables. "Justine, honey. Grab the cinnamon rolls and drinks from inside the food truck, would you?"

The young woman with a cute baby on her hip was Linc's little sister and the youngest of the Fortune Maloney siblings. The one who lived here in Rambling Rose. She handed off the baby to Linc and hurried into the food truck.

"I'll go and help," Isabel murmured, feeling decidedly third-wheel despite the look Reeve sent her way.

She walked around the tables and stepped up inside the food truck. What she knew about them would fit on the head of a pin, but the inside of Mariana's looked impressive. "I thought an extra pair of hands might help," she told Justine.

Justine quickly nodded and slid open one of the window coverings just enough to peek out. Isabel wasn't sure if she was more concerned about her baby or Mariana, who was exclaiming over the photo album that Gigi had produced. "How old's your little boy?"

"Morgan is twenty months."

"He's a cutie, that's for sure."

Justine smiled and began moving enormous glazed cinnamon rolls from a cooling rack onto a serving plate. "He's the spitting image of my husband," she said. "I can't *believe* the resemblance between Mariana and Gigi," she admitted in a quick whisper. "If they weren't right next to each other, I'd have never seen it."

Isabel grinned. "I saw it, too."

Justine blew out a breath and handed two filled plates to Isabel along with a bunch of napkins that she tucked under Isabel's arm. "Take those out. If I know my brothers, everyone will be glad to have something to do with their hands. I'll bring the drinks."

Isabel carefully carried out her assignment, managing not to spill the rolls or lose the napkins. When she was done, Reeve latched his hand around her wrist and tugged her down on the picnic bench beside him. As if for good measure, he dropped his arm around her shoulder.

She got the hint. *Stay put, Issa.* She reached for a napkin and placed one of the fragrant rolls on it.

Mariana had set aside the photo album and was looking at a black-and-white photograph of the Stellar house. "It looks so…normal," she murmured.

"It *was* normal," Gigi assured. "It was one of Grampy's favorite places in all of Chatelaine."

"I'm sorry we can't tell you more about what happened after Luz moved away," Reeve added.

Mariana shook her head. "This is more than I—" She broke off, clearly too moved to speak.

"Mariana," Harrison said after a moment. He licked a dab of glaze off his thumb. "Why *have* you been so certain that Walter was your grandfather? I understand why you knew it wasn't Wendell—" he gave an acknowledging nod toward Linc and the others "—but why Walter, specifically? He had two other brothers. Was it just based on information that Martin knew from Wendell?"

Isabel felt Reeve stiffen and she set her hand on his thigh. He covered it with his.

"Partly. But I also did my own checking. And my DNA has the same markers as Walter's other grandchild."

Reeve sat forward so abruptly, the glass of tea that Justine had poured for him nearly tipped over. "*PJ?*"

Isabel deftly caught the glass and moved Gigi's photo album out of harm's reach.

"Philip Jr.," Mariana confirmed, and sent Gigi and Reeve a look that was not quite apologetic. "When I didn't get any response from you, I ended up searching further afield. He, um, well, he seemed to take a sort of perverse pleasure when he agreed to having our DNA results compared."

"DNA testing usually takes time," Harrison said. Still thoughtful. Still reasoned.

"You don't know PJ," Reeve said grimly. "He's had to pull out his DNA profile more than once."

Gigi nodded. "People have been claiming they were Fortunes ever since I can remember." She was sitting next to Mariana. "How did you know how to reach him, though? He and *Maman* have lived in France for years."

"Martin," Mariana said, as if the answer was obvious. The others nodded.

Harrison looked thoughtful. Gigi and Reeve just looked stymied.

Isabel idly opened the photo album. It was the kind with a single snapshot per page and the first one was the same shot of Walter Fortune that had been hanging in the Chatelaine museum. "How did Martin enter the picture, anyway?"

Justine was playing patty-cake with Morgan. "I knew him from our local coffee shop," she explained. "He was a regular there, only it turned out that he knew my—" she glanced around at her brothers "—*our* grandfather." Her cheeks pinkened. "When he mistakenly thought I was marrying Morgan's daddy just for security, he admitted that he was Wendell Fortune's best friend and that we were all heirs to a secret silver mine."

"It was quite a scene," Linc said, and his brothers all nodded in agreement.

"Why would it be secret?" Reeve's voice was a little sharp. "That's what Wendell did. Helped run the family's silver mining operation alongside Walter."

Justine's lips parted slightly. "Honestly, I don't really know. What I do know is that Martin gave me a whopping huge check that was definitely real when I deposited it in the bank."

There was general assent among her brothers.

"He talked about the red tape he had to get through," Max added. "That's one of the reasons why we were all receiving our bequests at different times."

"What else do you know about this Martin Smith?"

Justine immediately bristled. "I know he's a very dear old man," she said firmly. "He's certainly cared more about our family than—" Her lips suddenly clamped shut.

"Than *our* dad," Damon finished. He was the youngest of the brothers.

"And he lives here in Rambling Rose," Harrison pressed.

"Except when he's in Chatelaine." Cooper was tearing apart a cinnamon roll with relish.

"At the castle," Max added.

Reeve pushed aside his own roll and leaned his arms on the table. "He met you at Fortune Castle?"

The others were looking at him as if he were dim. "Yeah," Max said. "Castle. Turrets. Armored suits. All that."

"Oh for—" Reeve bit off a curse. "I should have

figured." He looked at Isabel. "Smitty. *He's* Martin Smith." He looked back at the others. "Eighties? Gray hair?" They nodded.

"Grizzled beard," Max added.

"That's him." Reeve swore. "Smith. Smitty. He wasn't even trying to hide it. I was just too oblivious to see what was right in front of my face!"

Isabel heard their agitation. But she was busy flipping from the picture of Walter as a young man at the front of the album, to the one of him as an old man at the back. At least she assumed it was Walter, because why would Gigi be carrying around one of Smitty? Yes, the man in the photo had more hair than the castle's caretaker. And no grizzled beard. But there was no question that he resembled the old man who'd waltzed her around the grand hall at the castle.

Fearing that she already knew the answer, she turned the album toward Justine. "Is that Martin?"

Justine glanced at the photo and started to shake her head, but then frowned. She squinted her eyes and angled her head. "Actually, I…maybe? He looks a lot like Martin."

"That's *Grampy*," Gigi said, looking just a hair impatient with Isabel's interruption.

Reeve was pinching his eyes closed. "I can't believe this," he muttered.

Isabel ran her hand down his back, helpless to stop the trainwreck unfolding.

"Believe what?" Mariana reached out to take the photo album from Gigi. "May I?"

Gigi waved her hand. "I brought them for you to

keep. All pictures of Grampy. I thought you might like them."

Mariana's eyes reddened. She patted Gigi's arm. "I do, honey. Oh, I surely do." She pressed the little album against her generous bosom. "Don't believe what, Reeve?"

He dropped his hand and Isabel caught the look that passed between him and Harrison.

"Smitty is Martin Smith," Harrison reiterated quietly.

"And Martin Smith is Wendell Fortune," Reeve finished.

He suddenly slammed his hand on the table and the glasses jumped once more. So did Morgan, who turned his enormous green eyes reproachfully toward him.

Justine stood up from the table and bounced him on her hip again. "Why would Martin lie about it? Why say he was just Wendell's friend if he's actually—" Her voice turned choked. "If he's actually our grandfather?"

"That is a very good question," Reeve said grimly. "And I for one would like the answer."

"Reeve," Mariana chided. "It's not like he's done anyone any harm." She gestured around the table. "All he's done is share his good fortune. Unless there's something illegal about it all, I'm not sure I see the problem."

Isabel saw it, though. "It's just one more secret," she said.

"And it's past time they stopped." Reeve looked at the others. "This isn't about money. Not for me. If I've given you that impression, I apologize." He looked at Mariana. "And it's not about welcoming anyone into the Fortune fold. It's about integrity and doing what's right. As far as I'm concerned, Wendell needs to explain himself. The man is supposed to be *dead*."

"Then let's get him to explain himself," Mariana said easily. "Justine, honey, you give him a call. We all know he's got a Texas-sized soft spot for you."

"Right. Right." Justine handed off the baby to Linc again and pulled out her cell phone. She dialed it quickly and held it to her ear as she paced around the picnic table.

Isabel realized they'd begun garnering attention from the other marketplace shoppers. "Reeve," she said under her breath. "Maybe this isn't the best place to continue this discussion."

He muttered another oath, glancing around also and catching someone directing their cell phone toward their group, obviously taking a photo.

Justine lowered her phone. "He's not answering."

"He hasn't answered my calls either," Harrison said. "I've been trying for weeks."

"Get him to come to you," Isabel suggested, earning the focus of everyone else.

"How?"

She lifted her palms. The answer seemed so obvious. "Tell him something's wrong at the castle."

Chapter Sixteen

They all agreed to reconvene the following Saturday at the castle.

It wasn't as quickly as Reeve wanted, but the ones who deserved answers from Wendell even more than he wanted them were Justine and her brothers. All of whom had lives that didn't necessarily allow for dropping them at a moment's notice.

"Consider it a lesson in patience," Gigi had told him. "It's something we both need."

To counteract the desire to go to the castle before then and retrieve that last journal they'd discovered—which felt increasingly critical considering the information that Cora had unearthed about Walter and Wendell's gold mining venture—Reeve spent even more time at the office.

Until Cora threw up her hands in disgust with him

in the middle of the week. "You're making everyone in this office crazy," she bellowed at him. "Go play basketball or something."

He hadn't been to his usual pickup game since he'd aided Isabel's marital escape. He had no desire to see Trey, but a hard-charging game was probably just the ticket to get his mind off Isabel. Off Wendell and Walter and all the rest.

And if he managed to foul Trey a time or two, it wouldn't bother Reeve much.

The other man wasn't there, though. "Didn't you hear?" Hector dribbled the ball between his legs, keeping Jerry—another one of their regular players—from stealing it. "The old man sent him to work at their office in Florida. Wants him out of Texas for a while."

"Don't know why." Jerry finally got the ball, faked left and hit a basket. "Wasn't doing anything the rest of us haven't done."

"He got caught," Hector said. He leaned his hands on his knees, catching his breath. "That's what he did wrong."

"He got caught and he blamed Isabel for it," Reeve said flatly. And if Trace had sent him away, maybe the man had more sense than he'd thought. "If you're gonna marry someone, have the decency not to cheat. And if you can't refrain, then don't get married." He caught the ball from Marco and ran it down the court, slamming it through the net. Then he jogged to the bench and grabbed his gear.

"Where you going?" Hector's voice followed him. "You just got here!"

He threw the strap of his bag over his shoulder. "To see someone who smells a helluva lot better than you do."

Catcalls followed him out of the gym.

He showered and called Isabel when he was in his car. It was already late in the afternoon. "How about that sail? We can get it in just before sunset."

"I'd love to, but aren't you in Corpus?"

"I'll meet you at my place at the lake. And don't worry. Trey's been banished to Florida."

"How do you know that?"

"Guy gossip," he said. "See you soon."

He beat her to the lake. Which gave him enough time to borrow the sloop from his neighbor. He was just placing an ice chest in the boat when Isabel appeared. She was wearing denim cutoffs and a red shirt, her hair swinging around her shoulders as she sketched a wave and smiled. Her step quickened.

He didn't even realize he was pressing his fingers against the center of his chest until she skipped down the dock and held out her hand to cross into the boat.

He took it, then wrapped his arm around her waist and lifted her off her feet, lifting her across instead.

She caught his shoulders, her eyes dancing. "Hi." She sounded breathless. "Like the shirt."

He snorted. He wasn't wearing one.

He showed her where to sit while he cast off. They had a few hours yet before sunset and in no time at all, they were out in the middle of the lake with nary a soul nearby. The wind was practically nil, and the lap of the water rocked the boat gently.

She looked back at the shore. "Are we going to have enough wind to get back? Or is it a swim or row situation?"

"There's a motor if we need." He flipped open the ice chest and pulled out a bottle of champagne.

Her eyebrows went up. "Drinking and sailing? Is that allowed?"

"I'm not going to get drunk, and I won't tell if you won't." He popped the cork and filled two plastic flutes that he'd stored in the cooler. There was a small cabin below, but if he knew his neighbor, it would be a mess as usual. He handed one of the cups to Isabel and nestled the bottle back into the ice.

She tucked her dark hair behind her ear. She had a little gold loop earring that made him want to kiss her golden earlobe. Other than the earrings, her only jewelry was that delicate little infinity loop on her middle finger.

"What are we celebrating?" she asked.

"As long as it doesn't involve Wendell, Walter, castles, my family or aborted weddings, I don't give a flying damn."

Her smile widened. "That might leave us with nothing to talk about."

He tapped her cup. "I think we'll manage."

And they did.

They talked about anything. And everything. She

even admitted that she really didn't like champagne all that much, though she appreciated the gesture.

Her cheeks were so pink when she admitted it, he just laughed and tossed the $300 bottle carelessly back into the ice chest. Then he went down into the cabin—which was *not* as bad as he'd expected at all—and pulled two sodas out of the locker.

He refilled their cups and she turned and rested her back against his chest, and they watched the color blaze across the sky. Then she threaded her fingers through his and just like that, tension grew until it was a palpable thing.

He closed his eyes. Reminding himself that he was a grown man. He knew how to exercise self-control. He'd been doing it—

She suddenly turned in his arms and her dark gaze roved over his face. When she pressed her mouth greedily against his, self-control was the last thing on his mind.

"I didn't plan this," he warned, even though every cell inside him argued the point.

"Neither did I." Her hands roved over his shoulders. Her lips curved and she leaned up, pressing her lips against his jaw. "Okay, that was a lie," she whispered when she drew near his ear. "Maybe not planned, but definitely," her words went breathier, "definitely thought about." Her fingertips pressed into his biceps. "Did you?"

He let out a laughing groan and lifted her until she straddled him. "What do you think?"

Her inhale was a hiss and her eyes fluttered

nearly closed as she slowly rocked and her exhale was his name.

He caught her face in his hands and rubbed his thumb across her lower lip. Her lashes lifted and those warm brown depths invited him to dive in. Then her hands slid slowly down his arms. Found his.

"Touch me," she breathed, pulling his hands beneath her T-shirt.

Her breasts were warm and bare and taut. When he drew his thumbs across her tight nipples, she moaned sweetly and rocked even more deeply against him. "Can we do this right here?" She reached between them. Her fingers covered his length. Curling. Cupping. Wanting.

He would have told her they could do anything anywhere as long as she didn't stop what she was doing. But some kernel of sanity still existed and he managed to set her away from him long enough to stand up from the cushions where they'd been sprawled. He took her hand and pulled her down into the cabin. They might have been giddy teenagers considering the speed at which they yanked off their clothes.

And then she stood before him, breathless and exquisitely female, her body glazed in gold by the fading light.

"Beautiful." His throat felt tight. His voice hoarse.

"You're the one who is beautiful." Her fingers lightly traced his face. His shoulders. As hasty as they had been, she suddenly took her time, maddening him until he hauled her close and tipped her off her feet onto the bunk.

She laughed and gasped and then clung as he sank into her and everything that was unsettled inside him suddenly found its place. Its purpose.

The need to hurry banked.

Now it was all pleasure. All her.

Wood creaked.

Water lapped.

He drew their linked hands above her head. Her eyes, dark and lustrous, gleamed up at him. She whispered his name and slowly curled her legs around his as she arched taking him deeper and deeper still until the only thing his senses knew were her.

Isabel.

Whose touch surrounded him. Soothed him. Until hurry inevitably returned. Need deepened. Then she was tightening around him, his name on her lips as she shuddered and finally, finally he let himself just go.

It was dawn when he woke.

Her legs were still tangled with his. Her hand clasping his to her breast.

Sound asleep. Giving an occasional soft little snore.

He kissed her bare shoulder and she rolled away murmuring thickly.

He managed to decipher *five more minutes* out of that and smiled ruefully. If he laid there with her for *two* more minutes, she wasn't going to get any more sleep at all.

He slid off the narrow bunk and pulled a striped beach towel out of the cargo box, settling it over her beautifully bare backside.

Then he dragged on his cutoffs, went topside and quietly dove off the side of the boat. The lake water was cold. Bracing. He swam around the boat long enough to work off some steam. When he climbed back in the boat, she was still sleeping.

As early as it was, the lake was deserted except for a pontoon far to the south.

There was still no wind to speak of. He propped the cooler behind him and stretched out his legs, watching the sky. He figured if he never moved from their little spot on the lake, he'd have lived a perfect life all in the span of one night with Isabel Banninger.

Eventually, she poked her head up through the hatch. She'd dressed.

She held out her hand. "We slept all night?"

He helped her out of the cabin. "All night."

"I can't, uh, can't believe it."

He could.

She scrubbed her fingers through her disheveled hair. "Don't suppose you've got coffee in that ice chest."

He smiled. Shook his head. "No, but there's some pretty close by at my place."

He attached the small outboard that sounded loud in the silence of the morning. They motored slowly back to the dock he shared with his neighbor. He dumped out the nearly melted ice from the cooler, secured the boat and jumped out. She kicked off her sandals and they walked through the sand until they reached the shoreline path. When she pulled her hand away from his, he glanced down at her. His stomach was already growling for breakfast. For her.

But the way her gaze went one way, toward his deck, then the other, toward the LC Club, told him there would be no breakfast after all.

"Yesterday was great," she began and he braced himself.

"But I really should really go," she finished. The fact that her voice was full of regret was at least something.

"Why?"

She pushed her hands into her pockets. In the pale morning light, her face looked like ivory, her eyes espresso-dark. "Reeve—"

"Too soon," he said when her voice dwindled to nothing.

She bit her lip, not answering.

Which was answer enough.

Reeve's name might have been the one on her lips when they'd made love, but the wedding she'd run out on was obviously still too fresh.

Then she reached up and slid her small hand around the back of his neck, tugging his head down toward hers. She stood on her toes and brushed her lips slowly across his.

He drank it in like a parched man drinks a droplet of water.

She went back on her heels, her lashes lowered.

"Good luck on Saturday. With all that stuff we agreed not to talk about."

"You should be there. You're the one who saw the truth first."

She shook her head. "It was only a matter of time. But this is your personal family business."

"If I said I want you there?"

Her gaze flickered up to his. It was her turn to ask. "Why?"

There was a dam built up in his chest. Holding back a lot of things. But a lifetime before her made it impossible to get them out. "You'll have a helluva *Chatelaine Report* afterward," he said.

She swept her hair away from her forehead. "I won't write about that."

"Even if I give you carte blanche?"

She pressed her lips together for a moment, looking away. Then she shook her head slightly, looking rueful. "You're a dangerous man, Reeve Fortune."

He didn't have a chance to tell her she was wrong, because she just gave him that smile that was uniquely hers and walked away.

He watched her until she was no longer in sight.

He finally turned and went home.

Reeve was the last one to arrive at the castle on Saturday. He parked next to the haphazard collection of cars and turned off his windshield wipers.

Fitting that the sky was dumping another summer storm on their world.

He didn't bother with an umbrella and it felt

strange going through the front door when he'd spent two decades using the side. A dozen faces turned his way when he walked into the elaborate foyer, dashing raindrops from his hair.

Gigi hurried forward to buss his cheek with a quick kiss. This affection she was showing lately was taking some getting used to. But he decided he didn't really mind.

It was perfectly obvious that everyone there was paired off, except Mariana Sanchez.

Or was she already calling herself Mariana Fortune?

She had the right. So did the Maloneys. He hadn't thought about it much, but the fact that they were all cousins of one sort or another was finally sinking in.

"The party grew," he told Gigi.

"Lots of newly engaged couples," Gigi said, and quickly introduced the newcomers. "Remi goes with Linc. Eliza's with Max, Alana is with Cooper and Sari is Damon's girl." The last was Stefan Mendoza, who was Justine's husband. The baby was not there. Probably just as well.

"I called Smitty on my way here," Reeve told them all. "Told him there was another leak." Nice of the weather to give a plausible excuse. Unfortunately, it just made Reeve think of Isabel. He hadn't seen her since the lake.

"Where should we wait?"

Reeve shrugged. "Didn't think that far."

Gigi's eyebrows rose. "That's a first." She turned and began issuing suggestions. "Those abbey benches," she told Linc and Cooper. "Let's take those into the ballroom." Without missing a beat, she looked back at Reeve again. "How long do you think it'll be before he shows up?" She looked suddenly worried. "He wasn't in Rambling Rose, was he? It'll be hours."

Reeve spread his hands. "Your guess is as good as mine."

"Don't worry." Harrison squeezed the back of her neck. "I'm going to go around and hunt up a few more chairs."

"There are several in the office," Max said. "I remember where it's located."

The two men walked beyond the ruby-carpeted staircase.

The rest of the women went into the ballroom. He could hear their hushed whispers about the grandness of it all.

He rubbed his chest.

"Heartburn?"

He looked over at Stefan. He dropped his hand. "No. You look familiar," he said truthfully. "But I can't—"

"Mendoza Winery," Stefan said. "We've handled Fortune Metal's annual shareholders' dinner for the last few years. Now I'm partners in Rising Fortune Brewing Company."

That's what he remembered. The shareholders' dinner was a giant snoozefest that he left in Cora's capable hands. "Great IPA."

The other man grinned. "We think so." He moved to one side when Max returned with a wooden chair that looked like it came from the Dark Ages. "Next time we do this sort of thing, we need folding chairs."

"Let's hope there is no next time."

"Next time for *what*?"

They all spun around at the querulous demand that came from the inner doorway that led back to Wendell's study.

Smitty.

Martin.

Wendell.

All rolled into one.

Justine and Mariana came out of the ballroom and Smitty seemed to shrink a little as he saw them. As if he knew, finally, that the jig was up.

Justine was the first one to approach him. She took his hands. "Why didn't you just tell us the truth?" Her voice was thick. "Grandpa?"

Wendell's eyes reddened. "It's not that easy to turn back more than half your life," he said gruffly. When Gigi entered the room, he paled noticeably. "Effie," he whispered. "You're Effie all over again."

"Let's sit down." Justine took his arm and led him toward the ballroom. "It was wrong of us to shock you like this. I should've known better."

They hadn't collected enough seats, so Gigi and Reeve stood near the mullioned windows. He noticed that there wasn't a single drip of water coming through them. He looked back at Justine and Wendell, who were sitting together on one of the benches, and his gaze collided with his great-uncle's.

"Told you I'd take care of it," Wendell said.

"A window leak is one thing," Reeve countered. "Lying to your family for the last—what, fifty years?—is another."

"You're right." Wendell's apologetic gaze worked around his grandchildren. "I spent a lot of time trying to escape the name of Fortune. I thought I was better off without any family at all. There was just so much pain. So much loss." His voice cracked. "But youthful conviction can grow into old doubt. Since getting to know all of you," he said as he touched Justine's hand with his shaking hand, "I've faced just how wrong I've been. It's too late for me and Walter. But it's not too late for all of you. Family is so much more important than I wanted to believe. Knowing all of you—there's hope for this family. Real hope."

"What about Edgar and Elias?" Reeve's voice was hard. "Aren't you forgetting them in all your talk of family?"

Wendell blinked slightly. "They're dead."

"Like we were told *you* were dead?"

Wendell struggled to his feet. He jabbed his finger into the air. "Don't stand there judging me, son."

"I'm not your son." Reeve jerked his chin. "Their father was your son." He lifted his arms and dropped them. "Hell. Maybe Rick Maloney is as much a fraud as you."

"Reeve." Gigi grabbed his arm and squeezed it hard. "You don't have to—"

He shook her off. "What happened with Cortezalita Drilling, *Wendell*? What happened to the gold?"

Wendell sat down with a thump. His words, when they finally came, sounded hoarse. "You know."

Not as much as he wanted. "How many other secrets are you keeping?"

"That's all. The gold profits—my share of it—it's what I've been giving them." Wendell nodded to his grandchildren, the Fortune Maloneys. "I just wanted more time with all of you. That's why I took so long to give it to you. Why I drew it out and—" He broke off, coughing into the handkerchief he yanked from the pocket of his blue work shirt.

Justine slipped her arm around his shoulder. "It's all right," she soothed. "Don't get worked up. We don't want you landing in the hospital again like last year."

"Reeve," Gigi said through her teeth. "Lighten up."

Wendell collected his breath. "I told you all it was a secret silver mine. But it was gold. Walter found it. And he made me his partner. Elias and Edgar—" He shook his head dolefully. "They were always too greedy. Too careless. Eventually they caught the scent of gold and they thought it was at the Chatelaine mine. They worked the men like dogs. Day and night in search of it. Walter warned them, but they didn't listen and—" He coughed again into his handkerchief.

Reeve swore inwardly when he saw flecks of blood on the white cloth. He raked his fingers through his hair. "Wendell. Slow down."

"No!" The old man's response was more spirited than any of them expected. "You wanted to know, well, now you'll know." His voice rose. "Fifty men died in that mine collapse! Fifty deaths that could have been prevented if Walter and I would've just told the truth about Cortezalita."

Max, who was sitting in the dungeon chair that he'd brought from the office, suddenly shot out of it like he'd been bitten. He touched the wood carvings on it. "Is *that* what all these patterns of fifty stood for?"

Wendell had subsided again. He covered his eyes with a trembling hand. "My penance," he whispered. "A constant reminder of what my family had done. Edgar and Elias blamed the mining foreman for the collapse. And Walter—he threw enough money around to make sure questions that should've been asked didn't get asked. Edgar and Elias sneaked out of town like the weasels they always were. Later, we heard they'd perished in a boating accident, but..." He shook his head wearily. "Everything about being a Fortune had turned wrong. Corrupt."

Gigi looked pale. "And that's why you left," she said.

"If the castle was your torment, why come back to it?" Reeve demanded. "Why pretend to be the caretaker? How long have you been doing it?"

"Near fifteen years." Wendell's words were half wheeze. "It was curiosity at first. To see if what I'd built had stood the test of time. Walter was gone. Philip. Effie." He shook his head. "But this castle remained." He looked up at the murals on the ceiling. "It wasn't all bad. Effie—" His eyes closed and he exhaled. "She designed the murals. She was always too fine—" His eyes rolled back and he slumped.

"Martin!" Justine caught him, trying to stop his slide off the bench, and Stefan jumped in, too.

Reeve swore and yanked out his cell phone, but saw that Harrison was already dialing 911.

All Reeve could do was wait.

Edgar and Elias caused the mine collapse.

And now, Reeve had caused Wendell's.

It seemed to take forever for the paramedics to arrive. When they did, they worked over Wendell for long, tense minutes. By the time they loaded him on a stretcher, the old man's eyes were fluttering open again.

The others were following the stretcher out of the great hall and Reeve sank down onto the dungeon chair, weak with relief. His fingers dug into the heavily detailed carvings of birds on the wooden arms. Fifty of them. He didn't need to count to know.

"Reeve." Mariana appeared beside him. Her expression was kinder than he deserved. "Martin's asking for you."

He breathed an oath. "Suicide by Reeve?"

"You're better than that," she tsked. "At least I'm expecting you to be. So get your butt out there and talk to that man. Or do you want to lose what could be your last chance?"

He went. The paramedics were clearly impatient to get moving, so Reeve gestured them out the door as he came up next to Wendell. "I'll follow," he said.

They started rolling him out, one of them holding an oversize umbrella over the old man. Wendell caught hold of Reeve's sleeve. "Where's Isabel?"

It was the last question he'd expected. And it was like a punch to his gut. "She's not here."

"My grandchildren will be fine," Wendell murmured. "They already learned you grab on to love with both hands when it runs into you."

Isabel had literally run into Reeve. The memory was permanently etched on him. "She's not ready," he told Wendell. "Three weeks ago, she was set to marry someone else."

"But she didn't, did she?" Wendell sucked in air from his oxygen mask as he was rolled around to avoid the splashing water from an overhead gargoyle. "I saw that wedding dress stuffed in the closet." He huffed. "Saw you two dance. And other things."

Reeve felt his neck get hot even though rain was pouring down on him. He stepped back long enough for the paramedics to load the stretcher into the waiting ambulance.

One of them climbed up with Wendell. "You can come," she told Reeve. "There's room."

"No," Wendell said. He was breathing easier thanks to the oxygen they were giving him, and he lifted the mask for a moment. "He's got someone more important waiting for him." Then he laid his gray head back again.

Reeve moved again so the ambulance doors could be slammed shut. Then with the silent red lights strobing the rainy sky, the ambulance departed.

Gigi joined him. She was holding an umbrella, too, trying pointlessly to shield him from more rain. "Justine told me he was diagnosed with congestive heart failure last year. Every day that they get with him is a gift."

"How'd you know that Harrison was the one?"

At first she was stunned by the question, then her eyes softened. "Because when he holds me, I know I'm home."

"Aren't you scared? Not saying you should be. Harrison's a good guy. Even I can recognize that."

"You're a good guy, too, Reeve. You've just been too busy trying not to be like PJ while being busy trying too much to be like Walter. Maybe somewhere in the middle is a healthier place to be. And that's where I think you really are. Listen to Wendell. Go. I know that's what you want to do."

Isabel stared at the blinking cursor on her computer screen. "Please accept," she typed for about the fifteenth time before her fingers wouldn't type anymore.

Delete Delete.

"The *Chatelaine* reporter at work?"

She jumped and whirled around to see Reeve. His hair was wet. His clothes were wet. He was making a glorious puddle on the floor and everything inside her crowded up into her throat. "You're supposed to be at Wendell's Folly."

"I was. There's less folly than we thought. You should have been there."

She shook her head and turned back to face her laptop. She'd come to use the internet at the Stellar Productions building because she still hadn't gotten hers hooked up again at the apartment. It was stupid the way she kept putting it off. "That meeting needed to be family. Fortune family."

"You could be Fortune family."

Her heart squeezed and her fingers trembled on the keys, earning her a stream of gibberish on the screen. "You don't mean that." Delete. Delete. "I was writing my resignation letter. The ultimate irony, right? You give me carte blanche to write about your family, and I realize that I can't."

"What are you going to do then?" He leaned against the table next to her, his arms crossed over his chest. His shirt was so wet, she could see his skin right through it. It was a wonder he wasn't steaming.

She trained her eyes back on the screen. "There's always GreatStore," she muttered. "Always hiring."

"You're a writer. You told me yourself."

She clenched her jaw, remembering exactly what she'd said. Where she'd said it. What he'd been doing. How he'd smelled...

She deliberately typed again. "Please accept this—"

"What about writing something else?"

"That's what I'm *trying* to do!"

"Like Walter Fortune's biography?"

Her fingers trembled on the keys and she looked down at what she'd typed.

A;sdf9awue[tij;fdk

Gibberish.

She looked up at him. "Don't joke about that."

"Trust me. There's nothing funny about Walter Fortune's life. Wendell can help fill in the blanks. Which may mean you'll have to work fast. I am not sure how much time he's going to be around."

"Back to Europe, I suppose."

He shook his head. "He collapsed at the castle." He spread his palms, looking down at them. "My fault. Regardless of what condition his heart is in, I was the one who pushed him to explain. To tell us why he'd been lying to everyone."

She pushed back her chair. "What'd he say?"

"That being a Fortune was a curse. Maybe he's right."

She couldn't help herself. "You're not a curse. You're—"

His blue gaze caught hers. "I'm what, Isabel? Like Walter? I pulled my company's campaign contributions to Trace Fitzgerald—who is a pretty decent guy as a general rule—because of the actions of his son!"

"You think you're the reason Trey dropped that stupid business about making me pay for half the wedding expenses?"

"Yeah."

She shook her head. "Well, maybe it had something to do with it," she allowed. "But I had the picture, Reeve. The one of him and that girl. I'd saved it. And I told him if he didn't go away and leave me in peace, I'd put it on my blog." She raised her hand to stop his objection. "Now, I know my circulation isn't usually that big. But soon as I mentioned I was getting married to TFIII, it skyrocketed. Diana even got contacted by a few national networks. She said they were salivating for anything pertaining to Trace Fitzgerald's family."

"You didn't tell me that."

"You didn't tell me what you'd done either!" She reached up and slowly pushed his wet hair off his forehead because she couldn't seem to keep her hands off of him, no matter how much she tried to stop herself. "For the CEO of FortuneMedia, you're not exactly on top of things, you know."

His eyes crinkled slightly. "Maybe *that's* what you should do. Help me run it."

"You don't need me."

"I need you for a lot more than my company." He took her hand and pressed it to his chest. She could feel his heart racing. "I love you, Isabel. And I can tell you that I have *never* said that to another person in my life. The best thing that ever happened to me was you running out of that church, and I didn't even know it at the time." His hand squeezed hers. His eyes seemed to look down into her soul. "I know you think it's too soon, but—"

"I love you, too." The words came so easily. So certainly. As if they'd been part of her for her entire life.

He was staring at her and the leap of hope in his eyes would have made her fall all over again. "I love you," she said again. "Not just for now. Not just for tomorrow. For always."

"Then what do you think we should do about it?"

She reached up and wrapped her arms around his neck. His arms came around her and cradled her close and everything that was right in the world settled right there in her heart.

"First," she said as she brushed her lips against his, "I think you should call me Issa."

Epilogue

No man had ever looked so perfect. He wore a gray suit. Silver tie. Because, well, he was the Fortune silver guy. And he was all hers.

The way his gaze latched onto hers as she slowly walked toward him where he stood near the long pond told her everything she needed to know.

The hem of her dress—cream-colored, long-sleeved, scoop-necked, and chosen with the help of her mom and sisters—skimmed the autumn leaves that had just begun falling from the trees that week.

Nature, the most excellent stylist, had thrown vivid sprays of oranges and yellows and reds all around them. Behind Reeve, the pond glimmered almost as blue as his eyes that followed her every move.

She reached him and handed the clutch of wild-flowers that Reeve had picked himself for her just that morning to Ronnie, along with her great-grand-mother's prayer book with Granny Sophia's hanky tucked inside.

Then she turned to Reeve and placed her hands in his. Standing alongside him as his best "man" was his sister, Gigi. She gave Isabel a quick wink.

A photograph of Granny Sophia sat on the weath-ered bench nearby, alongside photos of Walter Fortune and Effie.

Loved ones lost, but never forgotten.

Sitting on a newer bench next to it was Wendell. Grizzled beard trimmed down to a nearly presentable scruff. Gray hair slicked back tidily and a black suit in place of his usual blue work clothes. Cora sat beside him, doing her best to look irritated by the way Wendell kept slipping looks her way.

Everyone else stood. There weren't a whole lot of them. Isabel's family. Reeve's new cousins and their families, and Mariana who was already dabbing the corners of her eyes and blowing her nose.

The weather was perfect and the only thing bluer than the October sky were Reeve's eyes as they said their vows and slid gold rings where it was so obvious they belonged.

Even Auntie Pearl looked misty when the minister pronounced them husband and wife.

After the newly married finally broke apart from a kiss that left the bride blushing and the groom grinning, the small crowd trooped back to the castle where—thanks to Isabel's mom and sisters—the great hall was finally bedecked in the finery that Wendell had always envisioned.

While the guests went inside, Isabel and Reeve lingered outside.

"Happy?" he asked.

"Extremely. You?"

"Supremely." He leaned down and brushed his lips over her cheek. "We could slip up to the Gold Suite," he murmured. "Start the honeymoon early."

She laughed softly. "We started that months ago," she reminded him. They'd only waited four circumspect months before saying their vows because Isabel had admitted to Reeve that her favorite time of year was autumn, at which point he'd tasked Cora with following the weather to choose the most colorful day they could find.

"We should probably go in and have our first dance," Reeve murmured. "One step closer to having you to myself."

She traced the swirl of ovals and ivy that was engraved on the door frame. To Wendell, they were symbols of penance. To Isabel, they were a promise of the years to come with Reeve.

He tugged her inside, and with her heart full, she joined him. Soon, they were sweeping around the great hall in each other's arms as the music spilled throughout the foyer and beyond.

None of them heard the soft thud of the big door as the wind nudged it shut. There was too much happiness inside. Too much love.

Whatever the world outside held, those inside knew what mattered most.

But outside?

Outside, the breeze tugged at the edges of the small note hammered below the heavy doorknocker.

There were 51.

* * * * *

Catch up with the rest of
The Fortunes of Texas: Hitting the Jackpot

Look for
A Fortune's Windfall
by USA TODAY *bestselling author Michelle Major*
Fortune's Dream House
by Nina Crespo
Winning Her Fortune
by Heatherly Bell
Fortune's Fatherhood Dare
by Makenna Lee
Self-Made Fortune
by USA TODAY *bestselling author Judy Duarte*
and
Fortune's Runaway Bride
by New York Times *bestselling author Allison Leigh*

Available now wherever
Harlequin books and ebooks are sold.

#2989 THE MAVERICK'S SURPRISE SON
Montana Mavericks: Lassoing Love • by Christine Rimmer
Volunteer firefighter Jace Abernathy vows to adopt the newborn he saved from a fire. Nurse Tamara Hanson doubts he's up to the task. She'll help the determined rancher prepare for his social service screening. But in the process, will these hometown heroes find love and family with each other?

#2990 SEVEN BIRTHDAY WISHES
Dawson Family Ranch • by Melissa Senate
Seven-year-old Cody Dawson dreams of meeting champion bull rider Logan Winston. Logan doesn't know his biggest fan is also his son. He'll fulfill seven of Cody's wishes—one for each birthday he missed. But falling in love again with Cody's mom, Annabel, may be his son's biggest wish yet!

#2991 HER NOT-SO-LITTLE SECRET
Match Made in Haven • by Brenda Harlen
Sierra Hart knows a bad boy when she sees one. And smooth-talking Deacon Parrish is a rogue of the first order! Their courtroom competition pales to their bedroom chemistry. But will these dueling attorneys trust each other enough to go from "I object" to "I do"?

#2992 HEIR IN A YEAR
by Elizabeth Bevarly
Bennett Hadden just inherited the Gilded Age mansion Summerlight. So did Haven Moreau—assuming the two archenemies can live there together for one year. Haven plans to restore the home *and* her broken relationship with Bennett. And she'll use every tool at her disposal to return both to their former glories!

#2993 THEIR SECRET TWINS
Shelter Valley Stories • by Tara Taylor Quinn
Jordon Lawrence and ex Mia Jones just got the embryo shock of their lives. Their efforts to help a childless couple years ago resulted in twin daughters they never knew existed. Now the orphaned girls need their biological parents, and Jordon and Mia will work double time to create the family their children deserve!

#2994 THE BUSINESS BETWEEN THEM
Once Upon a Wedding • by Mona Shroff
Businessman Akash Gupta just bought Reena Pandya's family hotel, ruining her plan to take it over. Now the determined workaholic will do anything to reclaim her birthright—even get closer to her sexy ex. But Akash has a plan, too—teaching one very headstrong woman to balance duty, family *and* love.

Get 4 FREE REWARDS!

We'll send you 2 FREE Books plus 2 FREE Mystery Gifts.

FREE Value Over **$20**

Both the **Harlequin® Special Edition** and **Harlequin® Heartwarming™** series feature compelling novels filled with stories of love and strength where the bonds of friendship, family and community unite.

YES! Please send me 2 FREE novels from the Harlequin Special Edition or Harlequin Heartwarming series and my 2 FREE gifts (gifts are worth about $10 retail). After receiving them, if I don't wish to receive any more books, I can return the shipping statement marked "cancel." If I don't cancel, I will receive 6 brand-new Harlequin Special Edition books every month and be billed just $5.49 each in the U.S. or $6.24 each in Canada, a savings of at least 12% off the cover price, or 4 brand-new Harlequin Heartwarming Larger-Print books every month and be billed just $6.24 each in the U.S. or $6.74 each in Canada, a savings of at least 19% off the cover price. It's quite a bargain! Shipping and handling is just 50¢ per book in the U.S. and $1.25 per book in Canada.* I understand that accepting the 2 free books and gifts places me under no obligation to buy anything. I can always return a shipment and cancel at any time by calling the number below. The free books and gifts are mine to keep no matter what I decide.

Choose one: ☐ **Harlequin Special Edition** ☐ **Harlequin Heartwarming**
(235/335 HDN GRJV)   **Larger-Print**
(161/361 HDN GRJV)

Name (please print)

Address   Apt. #

City   State/Province   Zip/Postal Code

Email: Please check this box ☐ if you would like to receive newsletters and promotional emails from Harlequin Enterprises ULC and its affiliates. You can unsubscribe anytime.

Mail to the Harlequin Reader Service:
IN U.S.A.: P.O. Box 1341, Buffalo, NY 14240-8531
IN CANADA: P.O. Box 603, Fort Erie, Ontario L2A 5X3

Want to try 2 free books from another series? Call 1-800-873-8635 or visit www.ReaderService.com.

*Terms and prices subject to change without notice. Prices do not include sales taxes, which will be charged (if applicable) based on your state or country of residence. Canadian residents will be charged applicable taxes. Offer not valid in Quebec. This offer is limited to one order per household. Books received may not be as shown. Not valid for current subscribers to the Harlequin Special Edition or Harlequin Heartwarming series. All orders subject to approval. Credit or debit balances in a customer's account(s) may be offset by any other outstanding balance owed by or to the customer. Please allow 4 to 6 weeks for delivery. Offer available while quantities last.

Your Privacy—Your information is being collected by Harlequin Enterprises ULC, operating as Harlequin Reader Service. For a complete summary of the information we collect, how we use this information and to whom it is disclosed, please visit our privacy notice located at corporate.harlequin.com/privacy-notice. From time to time we may also exchange your personal information with reputable third parties. If you wish to opt out of this sharing of your personal information, please visit readerservice.com/consumerschoice or call 1-800-873-8635. **Notice to California Residents**—Under California law, you have specific rights to control and access your data. For more information on these rights and how to exercise them, visit corporate.harlequin.com/california-privacy.

HSEHW22R3

HARLEQUIN
PLUS

Try the best multimedia subscription service for romance readers like you!

Read, Watch and Play.

Experience the easiest way to get the romance content you crave.

Start your **FREE TRIAL** at
<u>www.harlequinplus.com/freetrial</u>.